About the author

Throughout his career as a solicitor spanning more than four decades Charles Lander advised families on their problems — wills, trusts, tax and disputes — which he always believed would be fertile ground for stories derived from his experience. Once Charles retired, he decided to write about them and the result is this collection of stories, loosely based on fact.

Charles lives with his wife in south-west London, where they have lived for many years. They have two children and four grandchildren.

MY USUAL TABLE

Charles Lander

MY USUAL TABLE

Vanguard Press

A CIP catalogue record for this title is
available from the British Library.
ISBN 978 1 784659 70 7

Vanguard Press is an imprint of
Pegasus Elliot MacKenzie Publishers Ltd.
www.pegasuspublishers.com
First Published in 2021
Vanguard Press
Sheraton House Castle Park
Cambridge England

Printed & Bound in Great Britain

Dedication

To my family.

Chapter One
Leo

Leo, front of house manager at Messanto Restaurant, remembered the booking with little enthusiasm. Oliver Branscombe, a regular customer (or, to be exact, a regularly difficult customer) had called yesterday to demand that his usual table be made available for lunch today. The appointed hour was approaching and Leo was carrying out his last-minute checks in readiness. During his ten years at the restaurant Leo had dealt with many difficult diners, but Oliver Branscombe was in a class of his own. Leo's tactic, honed over the years, was to follow the diplomacy handbook and keep his welcoming smile firmly in place.

Leo had joined Messanto more by accident than choice. Leo was blessed with numeracy but had resisted all temptation and encouragement, from career advisers as well as his long-suffering parents, to join the accountancy profession. Just the thought of a regular job offering limited horizons had been enough to lead him, in his early twenties, to a more dangerous world, to a bank specialising in property finance. With hindsight, Leo now realised that the bank's business model had been guaranteed to fail if the economy stalled, but it had at least provided him with a good business sense and, no less important, a good income for ten years before the crash in 2008.

After the bank had folded, Leo's contacts had invited him to make an investment in a new restaurant which was opening, Messanto in Pimlico — not a traditional London area for restaurants, but not out of the way either. There were no plans to aim for Michelin Star status and he had readily accepted the invitation, and the offer to be a manager. Messanto was well situated: it was easy walking distance from the Tube and a short cab ride from the West End. Lunchtime refugees from the City came to Pimlico if lunch was to be extended to teatime and beyond.

The restaurant was renowned for its Italian food, well prepared and served with charm and efficiency. It occupied the ground floor space, oblong shaped, in an otherwise residential building. The décor was deliberately neutral in colour, the relaxed ambience set by a mix of natural light and carefully placed spotlights which could be dimmed easily — there was no overhead lighting. White tablecloths covered the tables, which were well spaced and set on a polished wooden floor. It could handle up to thirty covers at one time, with more space for fifteen at most in the private room at the back.

Leo had a good empathy with diners, conversation coming easily to him. Smart clothing suited him and, at just over six feet in height with a full head of hair, his presence was reassuring and added to the overall feeling of relaxed comfort. A couple of years ago he had recruited an assistant to help him, Julia, who had proved to be a great bonus. Her smile and sangfroid had proved more than a match for even the most recalcitrant diner.

Today, Thursday, was always a popular choice for lunch. Evening bookings were strong as well. Leo had helped to build a loyal clientele over the ten years: this despite the temptation — so far resisted — to tell some unappreciative diners they would be better served elsewhere.

Chapter Two
Oliver

Oliver Branscombe, who was approaching his fiftieth birthday, was by his own estimate a successful and charismatic City businessman. He would have liked to have been a few inches taller, coupling this with a brusque manner and a preference for conducting business when seated. It would have come as a surprise to him to learn that his approach created a charm-free zone.

His successes were marked by trips to Messanto and today's lunch was to celebrate the completion of a deal: yet another example in Oliver's eyes of his Midas touch, a description he liked to use too often for the comfort of those who worked for him, or for that matter against him. The restaurant was half full already, with more arrivals expected after one o'clock. The clientele was varied, including a young couple in one corner engaged in earnest conversation, an older couple arguing over the choice of wine and a local solicitor who had booked the private room and was waiting for his clients to join him. They and several others were regulars, a loyalty that enabled the restaurant to thrive and retain its staff.

With his smile cemented in place, Leo welcomed Oliver Branscombe and his entourage — Alison, his finance director, Douglas, his in-house lawyer and Lucy, his PA. Oliver's usual table was towards the rear of the restaurant, but in full view of restaurant reception in case some journalist or blogger was curious enough to see who was dining there. The fact that no visit of Oliver's to Messanto had ever attracted media attention had escaped Oliver's ego entirely.

Leo's welcome was dismissed by Oliver with a typically charming retort, "I hope you've got the Bollinger on ice, rather than that house rubbish you usually serve." Leo added the insult to his memory bank but showed no emotion as he guided the party of four to their table.

Leo was pleased to see that the regulars mostly ignored Oliver's arrival despite the commotion which accompanied it. The young couple looked up, exchanged glances with raised eyebrows and went back to their conversation.

Oliver had chosen his staff carefully, conducting the interviews personally to find just the right candidates. His interviewing technique owed more to abrasiveness than charm, but a smattering of the latter achieved what he wanted. Alison, who was in her late thirties, had joined him about three years ago from a major accounting firm, when she had realised that her partnership prospects were minimal. The offer to join Branscombe Bank had been well timed. Douglas, who had just turned forty, had joined a few months after Alison, realising that he preferred to meet the challenges of the bank than grasp the nettles of practice in a commercial law firm.

Oliver's opinion, frequently voiced, was that the three of them worked well together as a team: unsurprisingly, it was an opinion based on all team members doing exactly as they were told. Lucy had joined a few months before, Oliver having been attracted at her interview as much by her effortless elegance as by her impressive CV. She worked alongside him when deals were done, as well as completing more mundane tasks such as diary management and travel bookings.

The Bollinger was poured, and Oliver proposed his customary toast for a completed deal. "To the Midas touch". Glasses were raised, dutifully, but to say that feelings round the table were mixed would be a dramatic understatement.

Douglas had realised after the first few deals that Oliver and accurate financial records were strangers to each other. Douglas had no desire to end up on criminal charges.

Leo collected the menus once choices had been made. The sommelier allowed Oliver to select the wine, knowing from experience that it was simply a waste of time to make recommendations. He hid a smile when the selection proved once again that, when it came to choosing Italian wine, Oliver didn't know his Asti from his Alba.

Leo was then able to turn his attention to other diners.

Chapter Three
Henrietta

Leo went to the private room, where a party of four was expected. The solicitor host, Anthony, was from a firm renowned for its expertise in solving family problems. He had specialised in that kind of work for nearly twenty years and was an acknowledged expert in the field. The stress of this was beginning to show, as were more than a few grey hairs, and a furrowed brow was much more likely to be in place than a smile when he got home. He made frequent use of Messanto's private room and had confided to Leo that it was an ideal venue to hold gatherings, especially when family friction was likely. The more formal surroundings of a solicitor's office tended to emphasise problems, rather than solve them.

Anthony expected today to be particularly difficult. He was acting for a widow Henrietta and elder son Peter, the executors of Walter Hecht who had died a few weeks before. The executors were responsible for dealing with Walter's estate and passing it on to the family members as the beneficiaries of the will.

Anthony was joined first by Henrietta, a woman in her late sixties. He had acted for the family for some years. He had not been misled by her apparently understated approach to problems. He had found her to be an intelligent, determined but grateful client, willing to say please at the beginning and thank you at the end. The two of them ordered pre-lunch drinks from Leo, who then left them to a discussion that was not to be interrupted, even if the other family members arrived.

The discussion, which lasted some thirty minutes and was not their first on the subject, concentrated on how best to break unpalatable news which would have unfortunate consequences for the family as a whole.

Anthony emerged from the room to welcome Peter and his younger brother, Graham, his other guests for lunch. Relations within the family had always been strained, and the atmosphere in the private room was far from friendly. Peter and Graham exchanged perfunctory greetings — any warmth between them had long since been lost. Anthony sat at the head of the table in an attempt to control proceedings, with Peter to his right, Graham to his left. Henrietta sat at the end of the table, able to catch every facial expression round the table. Battle lines were clearly being drawn.

Peter, who was in his late forties, lived in commuter-belt Surrey with his wife Claire and their teenage children. He was intolerant by nature, with a drive to do more. Claire had declined to come to the lunch, knowing that her natural impatience would sour the occasion. "Just tell the bloody lawyers to get on with it, they'd lose a race with a snail given the chance," had been her parting shot as Peter left the house. For once, he agreed with his wife. Finances were strained to the limit, and an inheritance from his father would be more than welcome. His job as a PR consultant in a West End firm paid well, but not well enough to meet the demands of Claire and the children.

Graham was of a quieter disposition and had always felt overshadowed by his elder brother. Peter's drive and energy were in complete contrast to Graham's natural lethargy. The two-year age gap between them was not the problem — it was Graham's attitude to life, where no decision was really required today if tomorrow would do. Graham, who lived a life of comfortable chaos, was modestly paid for his work in an antiques business near to his home in Hampshire, but he was content. He had never married, not yet having met the right person, although an outside observer might say his efforts in that direction had been more hidden than visible.

The differences between the brothers were emphasised by their choice of clothing for the day. Peter, always neat if not dapper, had chosen a jacket, shirt and tie. Graham's choice had been less formal and matched his approach to life, his open-neck shirt saving him the trouble of wrestling with a tie.

Peter knew that his success was the result of his own efforts. Graham's success and contentment had been achieved despite his efforts, which Peter, even at his least irritable, found impossible to accept. Their mother's attempts to bring them closer together had foundered a while ago, when it had become obvious they would never be reconciled.

Graham had decided to join the lunch if only to remind himself of the gulf between the family members. Within seconds of arrival he knew the occasion would be more of an endurance test than a pleasure, but a dormant curiosity to learn a little more about the family, his father in particular, had been awakened. He sat opposite his brother and waited for the opening salvos to be fired.

Leo filled all the wine glasses and left the poisonous atmosphere with some relief. Anthony, aware that the family would find it difficult to agree even that today was Thursday, collected his thoughts and began.

Chapter Four
Oliver

Oliver held court. His courtiers listened, but their minds were elsewhere.

Douglas recalled the text message he had read on Oliver's phone a while ago. The message had pinged onto the screen as Douglas stood by Oliver's desk.

"Hi Oliver. Great deal. Usual arrangement? Alain". Douglas had dealt with only one Alain, a lawyer based in Monte Carlo whose clientele required careful scrutiny. Alain had taken it as a personal insult that his name had not appeared more in the Panama Papers disclosed a few months before. Despite regular business trips to Cyprus, Oliver had let slip little or no information about his offshore connections. Douglas' suspicions had been aroused by the cryptic message. Why was Alain involved and why had Oliver not told him? What was the usual arrangement?

Douglas had shared his doubts with Alison, who had been equally mystified. Oliver had dismissed their queries with a bland, "Alain means usual commissions and profit-sharing. You know all about it," and had refused to discuss the subject. It was within the offshore element that Douglas believed creative accounting was at work, but requests for more financial information about the offshore side of things had been met with an equally bland dismissal.

At the time, Alison had been more concerned with fending off Oliver's advances than applying her skills to creative accounting. For her, Oliver was at his most dangerous between deals, when his time wasn't fully occupied with business. No one seemed to know if Oliver had a wife, family or even a mother or father. His ability to dodge questions about this was well known and was second only to his attempts to seduce the female of the species (his description, much derided by the females of the species in the office). Rumour had it that Oliver was writing a book on charm and diplomacy: rumour also had it that the book would be too short to be worth reading.

She and Douglas were troubled by Oliver's attitude and reluctance to explain what was actually going on. Their offers to join him in Cyprus to meet the offshore investors had been declined less than politely. The dual shadows of Regulation and Compliance were always present, but Oliver's ability to gloss over regulatory hurdles was second to none.

Douglas and Alison had met one evening, at Messanto's, to agree a plan of campaign. The greater Oliver's reluctance to share information with them, the greater their curiosity. They decided information was the key, and agreed a strategy to find out more: they needed to find someone new to join the bank and get closer to Oliver in his business dealings, to add to the intelligence they might gather between them. The two of them needed help to do this.

Leo, ever helpful, had overheard snippets of their conversation. His dislike for Oliver was matched only by his wish to find out more. He had suggested they might need an employment agency. As chance would have it, the manager of the local agency was dining in the restaurant that very evening. The agency was known to Oliver and had introduced staff to the bank in the past.

Oliver's most recent PA had left abruptly only a few days before, with a parting sum considerably more than her contractual entitlement, a product of his activities between deals. They gave a brief to the agency to find a new PA for Oliver, capable of digging deeper than usual into Oliver's business life. The recruitment process had begun the following day and various candidates had been identified. Lucy had been interviewed shortly after and had started a month later.

Chapter Five
Henrietta and Walter

"Your father was a successful businessman, over the years turning a single shop into a major retail force with twenty or more high street stores". This wasn't news to the Hecht family, but Anthony needed to set a context. "He eventually sold out to a well-known chain of department stores, pocketing a considerable sum." Again, this was no surprise to the family, but Anthony's next words were in a different category. "Whilst building the business he'd been helped by a close friend, Natasha, and they worked tirelessly together to make a success of it. They became closer than friends, and married in the mid-1960s."

The two brothers sat completely still, dumbstruck by the news, but there was more to come. "They had a child within a year of being married, a daughter, Anne." Anthony knew he was condensing major events in Walter's life into a few words and so he paused for breath, allowing the brothers to take in what he was saying. "Your father and Natasha continued to build the business, but the increasing demands of a young child took their toll. Natasha felt trapped at home. Walter worked all hours and gave his family little support. The marriage broke up a year later and Natasha took Anne with her when she left."

Anthony paused again, to let the news sink in, and then continued his narrative. "Although the marriage had ended, Natasha was a staunch Catholic and wouldn't agree to a divorce. She was unshakeable about it. Natasha and Anne went to live in Northern Ireland, where they still are today and your father visited them from time to time. He also contributed to their upkeep throughout his life."

Neither brother uttered a word, even if the revelations produced differing reactions in them — the one suppressed anger, the other measured confusion.

Anthony took a sip of wine and pressed on before questions could be raised. "This all means that Walter was still married to Natasha when he died." The brothers looked at their mother, seeing a trace of apprehension in her face for the first time. Relief that the truth was out would come later for her, but her fear today was of a reaction, or overreaction, by her sons. Anthony had been alive to this, persuading Henrietta he should tell the full story and run through the consequences all at the same time. More detailed questions could follow later once her sons had thought about it. Realisation would dawn on the brothers that their parents had never married. Acting like the proverbial bastard is one thing, being an actual bastard quite another.

Henrietta's mind began to wander, recalling the past. She had meet Walter just after graduating from university. She had worked in Walter's first shop to get some money together for a trip round Europe, her last fling before beginning a more settled life. Although she had found Walter attractive, and suspected that the attraction was mutual, he was obviously in a relationship with Natasha that had more than business at its heart. He was also some years older than her, and she had been reluctant to try for more than a working relationship with him. Natasha's announcement she was pregnant had been the signal for Henrietta to leave for her trip. Her parents had supported her decision, agreeing she should broaden her horizons and further her education. Walter had made her promise to be in touch on her return, to work in the shop again because by then Natasha would have less time to devote time to the business.

Her trip to Europe had been planned with the help of her tutor at university, where she had read languages. He called the trip her last chance before the inevitable rendezvous with reality and had given her advice, such as 'you speak languages well, but please make sure you know how to say NO in every country you visit'. This resembled the advice offered by her parents before she left, but with a more practical bias.

The trip had taken her through France, into Italy and then on to Greece. She had taken in the sights, visited the museums and visited the long-lost cousins, but Mykonos had proved the most educational venue of all. Whilst there she had met a playboy restaurant owner, outlandishly attractive and the living, walking, talking — and tempting — embodiment of all that her mother had warned her about. He had pursued her with food, drinks and outrageous compliments, all in broken English which had somehow added to his charm. She had furthered her education over a few days in his villa, where he had expanded her knowledge of many things, including the local language — even to this day she could remember the Greek for temptation.

Reinvigorated by her experiences, Henrietta had returned to the UK and, after a couple of failed attempts to work elsewhere, had gone back to work in Walter's business. By then Natasha was facing the demands of motherhood, but with little support from Walter. He was concentrating on opening a second shop, larger than the first, and his efforts in that direction left him little energy or time to devote to his family. Little by little, argument by argument and flaming row by flaming row, their once loving relationship had deteriorated into an empty shell.

Henrietta had been caught in the crossfire, but had kept her thoughts to herself. Her affection for Walter had grown whist she was on her travels in Europe, and the decision to return to work for him had been easy to take. She was friendly with Natasha, who shared confidences with her — Natasha had admitted to Henrietta at the time that her pregnancy had been unplanned — but the three of them in such close proximity was bound to cause some stress. It had become increasingly obvious to Henrietta that, although Walter and Natasha were both to blame for the breakdown in their relationship, his drive for success had run so deep that it had become all-consuming. The damage was done before Walter had realised how serious it was. His failure for the second year in a row to come to Anne's birthday party, yet another symptom of the wider malaise affecting their marriage, had destroyed Natasha's confidence in her and Anne's future, and had been the final straw. The break-up had been inevitable and messy, Natasha returning to her parents in Northern Ireland, taking Anne with her.

It had been a natural process for Walter to rely more and more on Henrietta after Natasha's departure. He had turned to her for help when Natasha had refused him a divorce and had even admitted to a degree of guilt in causing the break-up. Their relationship had developed gradually, Henrietta being willing to bide her time for the man she loved. They moved into a flat together a while later and their relationship acquired the element of permanence that they both needed. Henrietta had accepted that she would never be married to Walter — for whatever reason he would not force the issue of divorce — and their life had progressed from there. They had both avoided the challenge of telling the full story to their children and the longer they had kept the children in ignorance, the more difficult it had become to tell them. Natasha was coming to Walter's funeral in a couple of weeks, bringing Anne with her. The children could be kept in ignorance no longer.

Which brought Henrietta back to today.

Henrietta heard herself say, "Let Anthony finish and we can then talk about it," a plea which was heeded by her sons.

Anthony pressed on. "You'll want to know what this all means for the family. Walter's will clearly states that his children should share equally once your mother has been fully provided for. That means Anne will get a share. The two of you will get one-third each, rather than the one-half you were expecting." Anthony glanced at the two sons — the one seemingly calm, the other obviously seething — and continued. "There's less in the estate than you think because of the amounts paid to Natasha and Anne. There's also a major tax problem. Your parents weren't married, which means that inheritance tax must be paid on anything Walter leaves to your mother. If they had been married there would have been no inheritance tax to pay." Anthony had saved the worst until last. "The inheritance tax rate is forty percent. Walter's entire estate will suffer tax at that rate. Overall, there'll be much less left for the family than you thought."

Anthony sat back in his chair, his unpleasant duty done. He could only imagine the conflicting emotions in his audience.

Chapter Six
Oliver

Oliver looked at his watch in the way impatient people have to show they'd prefer to be somewhere else. He was bored with the conversation. His lunch companions were equally bored, as Oliver had droned on about his past successes. Oliver was oblivious to this and failed to sense the relief at the table as he announced, "I must be making a move. Good lunch. Just use the company card to pay the bill would you Alison?" With these words he left the table, and the restaurant a minute later once he had checked his phone.

He hailed a cab, giving an address in Chelsea Wharf. The phone he had checked was his personal phone, paid for by him and quite independent of his office mobile. As he hoped, Sarah was at her flat. Her texts had also confirmed she was packing for their trip to Cyprus at the weekend. She had booked her flight and organised the taxi to take them to Heathrow early tomorrow.

As the cab headed down Chelsea Embankment in the afternoon traffic, Oliver reflected on his relationship with Sarah. They had met through business a couple of years ago. She was much the same age as him. Oliver knew she was a match for him in every sense. Her intellect matched his, and she was as impatient of others as he was. Her business acumen was every bit as keen as his. He admitted, if only to himself, that he lacked emotional intelligence, but Sarah more than compensated for that.

Most important of all, they shared the same flaw. Why share profits with others when you have done all the hard work? The trip to Cyprus was to ensure the fee-sharing for the most recent deal, the hostile but successful take-over of a company, was fixed in the usual way. The bank would receive a handsome fee in London for its work in putting the deal together. A special fee would also be paid to Oliver in Cyprus. Alain's offshore investors channelled their business activities through Cyprus and were from countries where 'commissions' such as those paid to Oliver were normal business practice.

Oliver was nostalgic for the unregulated business world which had prevailed at the beginning of his working life, which contrasted strongly with current thinking that even a moderate lunch was to be treated as a bribe. Everything was a question of degree, surely, a concept Oliver interpreted as generously as his conscience would allow. Boundaries were there to be pushed after all. He gave full value for money.

Sarah herself worked for the investors, identifying new business activities for them, and she had met Oliver when they had worked together on a deal. Their business rapport had been instant. Their sexual rapport had taken longer, but when it had surfaced it had taken both of them by surprise. The weekend trip promised to be a mixture of business and pleasure.

Oliver's wealth, both within and outside the UK, had accumulated nicely as deals in London had been in good supply: his Midas touch had not deserted him. He would discuss with Sarah over the weekend whether he might move from the UK. They had already discussed working more closely together, which was also shorthand for having a closer relationship.

It was with a sense of anticipation that Oliver paid off the cab and set off towards Sarah's flat.

Chapter Seven
Oliver

Lucy had proved to be worth her weight in gold in finding out what Oliver was up to. Although a canny businessman, his command of modern technology was basic at best, and the digital history of his documents and emails had been all too easily accessible. Lucy had been able to build up a dossier which did not make happy reading for Oliver. Or the bank. Oliver's secret commissions were traceable despite his efforts to hide them. Other commissions had also been paid to smooth transactions along, some of these to individuals who did not pass any business smell-test.

Oliver's actions were borderline criminal and so the facts had been reported to Action Fraud in London. Lucy had again proved invaluable in the process. She had discussed her concerns with her colleagues in the City of London Fraud Squad, to whom she would be returning as soon as the current investigation had been completed. She had been recommended as ideal for the task of finding out about Oliver's business activities. Her employment at the bank had been simple to achieve, given Oliver's monopoly of the recruitment process.

Her CV and appearance had been carefully crafted to appeal to Oliver.

In the spirit of full co-operation with the authorities, the bank's compliance officers and external lawyers would be meeting the Fraud Squad at the office tomorrow, when Oliver would be away on his long weekend.

On his return to the office next week, Oliver would be greeted by the external lawyers. The facts would be made clear to him. He would be invited to resign immediately. He would be warned of the police's involvement, through the Fraud Squad. He would be invited to refund the secret commissions paid offshore. He would be advised to get a lawyer, and quickly. Oliver would realise his arrest on criminal charges was imminent.

Chapter Eight
Peter

In the private room, Anthony had no sooner finished speaking than Peter had rounded on his mother. "Why the hell didn't you tell me all this before? It changes everything." His shrill voice had reached a crescendo as he berated Anthony too. "You're completely incompetent for allowing it all to happen. I'll sue you for every penny you've got."

Henrietta had decided beforehand to ignore the vitriol she expected from Peter, and she was not surprised at his failure to mention the impact on her or his brother. His selfishness of spirit had manifested itself from an early age, and was an aspect of his character which had fought continuously over time with the better side of his nature, before emerging triumphant by the time he had graduated from university. She looked at Graham, whose reaction was as much incomprehensible to Peter as it was a relief to her. "How do you feel, Mum? Must have been difficult for you to live with it." The contrast with Peter's thoughtless bravado was stark.

Ignoring a more conciliatory or tactful approach, Peter had stormed out, shouting that Anthony could expect to hear from his lawyers. Anthony had not risen to the bait, preferring to leave arguments of that kind to another day. The estate was already burdened with a huge tax liability, and to add more legal costs to the problems faced by the family would only reduce the value of what remained. It was difficult to see who would gain from it all, apart from HMRC.

Before the lunch, Anthony had revealed to Henrietta that Natasha had a claim on the estate, as a wife and someone for whom Walter had made generous provision in his lifetime. He had no idea if she would make a claim and the family could only wait and see. Henrietta, now aware of this, had agreed to keep the news from her sons and to tell them only if a claim was made.

Chapter Nine
Midas

Leo was reflecting on the day.

Peter Hecht had rushed past him without a word, leaving the restaurant as if pursued by demons. Henrietta had shared a drink with Graham, the two of them leaving together as if to prove not all mud that is slung finds a home on its target.

Oliver had left the restaurant in a hurry, but taking a cab in the opposite direction to his home in Holland Park. Leo filed this away in his memory bank as well.

Leo had one further thought. Oliver's obsession with his Midas touch betrayed an ignorance of the Midas legend. Although fabulous wealth was his because everything he touched turned into gold, Midas had discovered that in truth his touch was a curse. All his possessions turned into gold when touched. His family and friends would not go near him because, if they touched him, they would be turned into gold. All food and drink he touched turned into gold: he would die. He had been left with no alternative but to appeal to the Gods to lift the curse.

Leo looked at the bookings for the evening. An interesting set of diners, each with a story to tell. He would keep his eyes and ears open.

Chapter Ten
John and Cathy

John and Cathy Prowse were faced with a difficult dilemma, in fact more than one, which they had decided to talk through over dinner at Messanto. They were seated at their usual table, Leo having greeted them as regulars with his usual enthusiasm. Menus in hand, they were deciding what to choose before moving on to the main purpose of the evening.

John's life so far — he was in his mid-fifties — could best be characterised as safe. He was a man of average intelligence, average appearance and average ambition. As a result, he had been an averagely productive employee at a clearing bank for the last twenty-five years, working in the retail side of banking. He had risen (some said without trace) to manager level, defying the principle that each person eventually reaches their own level of incompetence. He was assured in his work, knowing when to pass on a problem (or the buck).

In short, he had proved an ideal and loyal employee for the bank. Developments in retail banking, not the least of which were branch closures and the increasing drive towards online banking, had brought some clouds across John's horizon. The personal contact with customers, such an important and enjoyable part of the service provided during his early years at the bank, had reduced to almost nothing, underlining the major shift from personal to impersonal banking.

John was not sure what his future role would be, but his uncertainty had been pre-empted by an offer for him to take early retirement. The bank's offer was a good rather than generous one, and he and Cathy were faced with their first dilemma — whether he should accept it.

Cathy had watched John's career with a mixture of pride and frustration. He was clearly valued by the bank but had lacked the imagination to adapt to the changing business world around him and to challenge for a different role. They had been together for almost thirty years, the last twenty as a married couple. She saw the offer of early retirement as an opportunity for the two of them to start a new phase in their lives. It was not that she was unhappy, she just wanted to be happier with her lot. Their only child, a daughter, would shortly leave home to go to the Far East with friends for several months, and was due to go to university after that. This would leave Cathy with a void in her life, one which she wanted to fill.

They had married and bought a mews house just off the Gloucester Road, where they had lived ever since. The mews had another ten houses in it, all freehold, and changes in ownership in the mews were rare. There was a strong community spirit amongst the owners, and an informal residents' association had emerged as a way to socialise and discuss common problems.

Both of them were tiring of the London life. The bright lights didn't seem quite so bright, and their visits to theatreland were fewer and further between. They had agreed long ago that they would move away from London at some time, almost certainly back to the Sussex coast where they had both spent their lives as children and where they had first met. Their parents — both sets — still lived there and were getting no younger. They paid regular visits to friends there, and the lure of the sea, with occasional sunshine, was increasingly attractive.

Following the bank's offer, they had decided to test the market and had put their mews house up for sale. If they sold at the right price, they could finally pay off the mortgage, buy a comfortable house on the coast and have enough left to live a comfortable life.

It was the decision to test the market which had presented them with their second, and greater, dilemma.

The estate agent handling the sale had proved reassuringly efficient. He clearly had instructions from above to move his firm up the public popularity stakes and, as part of this, had turned up for meetings well prepared, well dressed and on time. He was a born salesman, stressing his knowledge of the local market and how best to test it. At their first meeting, he had produced a sales brochure for 'Mr and Mrs John

Prowse', with a marketing strategy for 'this uniquely attractive and centrally located mews property', together with an analysis of recent sales in the area. The strategy had born fruit after only a couple of weeks, but in two very different ways.

One viewing had been set up by a property finder, whose job it was to find a London house for her client who was based in central Africa. Two further viewings, including a visit from a family member who had arrived in convoy with two personal security guards, had resulted in an offer to buy at £10,000 more than the asking price.

Other viewings had resulted in another offer, from a UK-based couple, but of £40,000 less than the asking price.

At first sight, the higher offer was the one to accept. The dilemma lay in the circumstances of the two buyers. Minimal desk research had revealed the African buyer to be of suspect provenance, with a history of exceptionally doubtful dealings in the markets. One prominent member of the family was under house arrest in Africa. Whether the mews house was to be a pièd-à-terre, or a refuge from foreign tyranny, remained to be seen. Added to this, the family member had revealed they intended to apply for planning permission to extend the house, both up into the roof and digging deep down into the basement.

The UK-based couple were more straightforward. They had already sold their house in the Cotswolds, having decided to move back to London after a failed farming venture. They were true cash buyers able to move quickly, but unable to increase their offer despite encouragement from the estate agent.

Having ordered their food, handed the menus back to Leo and chosen some wine, John and Cathy discussed their options. They were using a solicitor for the sale, whose advice had been to the point (if unsubtle). "It boils down to money," had been his candid view. "The African buyer has passed the financial tests we need at the moment and so it's your decision." The solicitor had discounted entirely the effect on the mews of a buyer such as the African family. Extensive building works would ruin the look and feel of the mews and would be opposed by the other occupants of the mews: a recipe for friction. The other occupants were keen to know who their new neighbours might be. John and Cathy understood this and knew they would find it far easier to reveal they were selling to the English couple. They had lived with their neighbours for many years and would far prefer to be able to look them straight in the eye in future, rather than leave a legacy of division and discord.

Whether John and Cathy were correct about how their neighbours would react, or had overestimated the reaction, or whether planning permission would be granted for the building works, was not the point. It was how they felt about it, and about their neighbours, that mattered to them. The problem, which looked insuperable, was the money. They could not afford the house they had found in Sussex, and live the lifestyle they would like over the coming years, unless they received at least the asking price for their mews house, preferably more. The owners of the Sussex house, which they had set their hearts on, were pressing for a firm commitment. Meanwhile, the house was to remain on the market. They were spending the coming weekend in Sussex, visiting parents but also searching for other houses they might buy. It went without saying — neither would admit it openly to the other — that they hoped the search would prove fruitless.

Procrastination was no longer an option for John and Cathy as they batted the dilemmas back and forward over tagliatelle and tiramisu. Regular attention from Leo in bringing just the right amounts of food and drink to their table, at appropriate intervals, had eased the conversation, but had brought resolution no closer by the time they had finished their meal, paid their bill and left the restaurant.

Leo's regular visits to the table had been no accident. He had understood the dilemmas and a plan was forming in his mind. He would make some calls, only too aware that if his attempts to put two and two together were to succeed, his answer needed to be more than four.

Chapter Eleven
Anthony & Co

The private room that evening had been booked by Anthony's firm, so that about ten partners could talk through issues affecting their firm. The legal world was changing constantly. They needed to innovate and to anticipate trends as best they could. If truth be told, the conversation itself in convivial surroundings, with excellent Italian food and wine, did as much to encourage the firm's success as did their attempts to second-guess the legal market.

The firm had fifteen partners at present, and measured expansion was part of the business plan. For some partners to gather every three months or so had been Anthony's idea initially and had, over time, become an integral part of the firm's calendar. A few months ago he had been elected as the managing partner of the firm. He had accepted the role and in his own mind wanted to disprove the maxim that some lawyers have greatness thrust upon them, the remainder go into management. His whole approach was based on communication, believing it was better to have an open disagreement than cloak-and-dagger whisperings behind his back. The private room encouraged tongues to be looser than would be the case in the firm's office building.

The age range round the table was the strength, although some considered it the weakness, of the firm. The predominantly youthful partnership still had some older partners, mostly male (and, if the support staff were to be believed, stale as well), who had shown a marked reluctance to retire, but clients of a similar vintage welcomed their input. Their contribution to clients was vital, although their mastery of modern technology did not register on any known scale.

Several different legal disciplines were represented round the table. Property and family (or was it divorce) work played a major part in the firm's success and were well represented. A couple of litigation specialists, each adept at starting an argument in an empty room let alone in Messanto's private room, kicked off the proceedings by announcing for the first time they were intending to expand their team (it was no longer called a department) by recruiting a partner and an assistant from another firm. They were well aware this would annoy their colleagues, but they could resist everything but the temptation to announce it that evening. There were usual channels within the firm for setting hares of that kind running, but why have them if they could be short-circuited by tonight's conversation?

The spark lit by the litigation partners became a flame as the conversation moved on to the firm's profitability. How could more partners be taken on unless the profitability was good enough? Anthony could have written the script for most of the contributions made to the discussion, but the lively exchange of views was a necessary part of legal life. The contrasting styles of the partners never ceased to surprise him, ranging from the measured approach of the lawyers dealing with wills and trusts to the confrontational style of the contentious lawyers, whose training required them to assume Humpty Dumpty was pushed and to sue as many of the king's men as possible.

Anthony allowed the discussion to run on, but empty vessels making the most noise was a phrase that sprang to his mind after a few minutes and so he moved the conversation on to the most pressing issue — the time was fast approaching when decisions needed to be made about the level of staff bonuses, payable with the December salary.

All around the table were aware of last year's disaster, when bonuses which the staff, correctly, had seen as measly and mean, had been followed swiftly by the New Year announcement of a record increase in the firm's profits, all of which had ended up with the partners.

The staff's reaction had been universally sullen, and had been summarised in a poem sent by anonymous email to all the partners:

> The bonus rears its ugly head
> There's not enough, or so it's said

To pay one half of last year's figure
And yet the firm gets ever bigger.
You must ensure that profits grow
And this I say just goes to show
That lawyers working as a team
Are large as life and twice as mean

The author of the email had been traced easily, as had been his intention all along. He was an assistant solicitor, disaffected for some time, who had just given notice to leave the firm for a competitor. His point had struck home forcibly with the partners, which had also been his intention. The consensus round the table for this year was to pay a substantial bonus to the staff who deserved it, which was another way of saying that final decisions could be taken later — who was to say who deserved it? It was also another way of saying, "Over to you Anthony."

Leo checked the room from time to time, knowing some partners had a greater capacity for food and drink than others. One particular partner merited special attention: his main aim in life seemed to be to test the regenerative powers of the human liver, and Leo was not going to allow him to flunk the test. Others also had no intention of dying of thirst, another plus for Leo. Food in sensible quantities had disappeared with gratifying speed, adding to the chef's reputation.

Leo's unobtrusive efforts ensured that a successful evening was underway, but he was waiting for another partner to arrive, Clive, who specialised in property work. He needed to catch his eye and have a quick word with him if he could. Leo had established that Clive was acting for the English couple who had made an offer for the Prowse's mews house and he needed to run some thoughts by him.

Clive was known for his timekeeping, or lack of it. If you wanted him to arrive at the right time, it was advisable to tell him an earlier start time than was actually true. Clive arrived after the meal had begun, but Leo had managed to speak to him confidentially for a couple of minutes before allowing him to join the others in the private room. Leo had been encouraged by the conversation, comparatively brief though it had been.

Chapter Twelve
Elizabeth

Once the meal had been finished in the private room, it was usual for one of the partners to entertain the assembled company with an anecdote about work, past or present. Tonight, was no exception and one of the family lawyers, Elizabeth, had drawn the straw, not necessarily short, to speak. She was a born storyteller and her story was from a time gone by. She drew breath, and began.

"My grandfather was a barrister, working in the Temple off Fleet Street. He was successful, known for his intelligence and his ability to think on his feet. He was a QC, well respected by his colleagues. He commuted to London each day from his home in West Byfleet, taking the train to Waterloo.

"My story comes from one such journey, in fact on the way home one summer's evening. In those days — we're talking about the late 1950s here — there were First-Class carriages and my grandfather had boarded the train at Waterloo, settling himself into the comfort of a First-Class compartment. I say compartment because there were no corridors on the train. Once you'd boarded the train you remained in the same compartment, it was impossible to move until the train reached its next stop.

"Having worked until after seven o'clock that evening, my grandfather hadn't boarded the train until about seven forty-five, which meant it was not as crowded as in peak rush-hour. It was still daylight and my grandfather had watched the houses of south London, still showing the scars of the Second World War, give way to the countryside. Times were hard for many and the streets of the city showed it.

"At the stop before West Byfleet the last passenger in his compartment had left the train, leaving him on his own. Or so he thought. From his window seat he had watched a young woman walk up the platform until she reached his compartment. After a moment's hesitation, as if facing a choice, she had joined him in the compartment, taking a seat diagonally opposite him.

"As the train pulled out of the station, he had taken a closer look at the woman. She was what his sisters would have described as 'cheap' — her blouse was a size too small, straining at the buttons, one too many of which was undone. Her skirt was slightly too short to be smart, and her face, caked in powder, was marked by a slash of lipstick. He had turned his eyes back to the window, knowing his home station was only a couple of minutes away.

"His attention had been drawn back to the woman by her chilling words, "Oi, you. You can afford it. Unless you pay me five quid, I'll scream blue murder at the next station and say you attacked me." Five quid was lot of money in the 50s, but an amount a passenger in a First-Class carriage might be expected to have in his wallet. You must remember that debit and credit cards didn't exist at that time — you paid by cheque, failing which cash was king.

"My grandfather had enough in his wallet to pay her, but his reply, as the train was approaching the station, was short and to the point. 'You can do what you like, madam, but I'm not paying you a penny.'

"She stared at him in disbelief for a moment, but realising the train was pulling into the station, she knew she had to act quickly. She flicked a V sign at him, then ripped her blouse, smudged her lipstick and powder and tugged at her hair, all blatantly designed to make it look as if someone had grabbed her. As the train came to a halt, she went to the window, already open to the summer air and, as threatened screamed blue murder. The platform guard came running, as did the train guard. The passengers on the platform were transfixed by what was happening.

"'What's the problem, madam? Are you all right?' were the obvious questions from the guards, to which the reply was as threatened.

"'That bastard attacked me a minute ago,' she said pointing to my grandfather. 'You can see what he's done to me,' she added, pointing to her blouse and face.

"All eyes turned to my grandfather, who throughout the turmoil had remained seated and apparently unmoved. His reply was scathing. "I did not attack this woman. I have been smoking a cigar since boarding this train at Waterloo. The ash on it is almost three inches long," which he proved by holding up the cigar, 'and would have fallen off if I had attacked her. I suggest you call the police whilst I decide whether to press charges.'

There was a moment of calm, before the guards turned towards the woman. She tried to bluster her way out of it, but the coup de grâce trumped her protestations of innocence. Subdued and now silent, she was led away to await the arrival of the police.

"The woman had later pleaded guilty at her trial. The case had attracted some publicity, which had encouraged several other men to come forward, saying they too had been victims of the woman's blackmail but had paid up. She had obviously been playing this particular game for several months and must have collected a tidy sum from her victims."

Nods of approval towards Elizabeth as she finished her tale brought the evening in the private room to an end. The partners then made their way home, some more steadily than others, having thanked Leo, some more vociferously than others, for his usual skills in making the occasion so enjoyable.

Chapter Thirteen
James

Leo was not at the restaurant when the lunchtime diners began to arrive that Friday. He was happy to leave lunch that day to Julia, whose efficiency had increased with every day. A few regulars were there, with some extras such as a couple of ladies finding time for a light lunch before resuming what was obviously a day's shopping, and a younger couple engrossed in conversation.

One regular, James, was at his usual table at the side, about halfway down the restaurant. James was proud of his stylish appearance. The cut of his suit suggested Savile Row, with a shirt and silk tie of similar quality. Urbane was the best description of him.

His education had been expensive, at a boarding school in a remote part of the West Country, good enough to teach him how to compensate for an intelligence that did not always match that of his contemporaries. His sporting prowess was formidable and, whilst passing exams was not his forte, his sales techniques enabled him to survive and thrive: buying up all available supplies of the most popular chocolate bars from local shops and then selling them on to his schoolmates at a profit had been just one scheme of many. The school had agreed with his parents that his future need not include a university degree and so he had left school immediately after passing one out of three A Levels, to go straight into the family business.

Charming could also be said of him, but at the moment James was turning on the charm in short bursts. He was experiencing the trauma of divorcing his wife on the grounds of her unreasonable behaviour, whilst at the same time trying not to admit his own appalling behaviour. If anything, his behaviour throughout the marriage had been so dreadful as to be beyond description, but the marriage had run its natural course and it was time, in his mind, to move on. At least there were no children to complicate matters.

With all the flair of someone bereft of strategic thought, and against his lawyer's advice — Elizabeth thought they should wait until they had collected more evidence — he had launched the divorce proceedings. His wife, Amanda, suspecting (not for the first time, with an instinct that had proved unerring so many times) that he was up to something, had frustrated him at every turn. Her patience had worn so thin over the ten years of their marriage that she no longer gave him any rope, even if there was a strong possibility he would hang himself with it.

It was an affront to Amanda that James was relying on her so-called unreasonable behaviour, and she was unforgiving. The combative side to her nature came to the fore, particularly when money was the main issue.

She delayed court hearings and cooperated to the minimum level necessary. Subconsciously over the years, she had learned well from her husband. If he suggested something, her defence mechanism was to oppose it, no matter how sensible it seemed. She didn't trust him and wanted to know what lay behind his thinking. Her curiosity, unsatisfied, kept her awake at night (as did her new lover, but that was a secret to be disclosed later, if at all).

James wanted help to see how best to get the proceedings moving, so that he could get on with his life. He possessed native cunning, but strategic planning was alien to him. There was to be a court hearing about the financial side of things in a few days and so he needed help urgently. Only then could he tell Elizabeth what to do about the hearing.

He was reluctant to confide in more than one or two close friends. A basic stubbornness in him meant he invariably left it to the last minute to seek help. To call a mule stubborn was to underestimate James: he would be king of mules if given the chance. His guest at today's lunch was his best man of ten years ago, Roger, who always gave sound advice and who was certain not to betray confidences.

Roger had lived through the ups and downs of the marriage and was well aware of the characters involved. James was camped at Roger's flat for the moment, having left Amanda in the matrimonial home. Roger had remained single, preferring the freedom of a bachelor existence to the rigours of marriage.

Once they had ordered they set about the task in hand, discussing tactics and weighing up options about what to disclose, and what not to disclose, at the impending hearing. They discussed James's relationship with another woman, which had failed only recently and decided that it would be dangerous to admit to it, at least at this stage. They discussed his precarious financial position. His family company, of which he was sales director, had been hard hit by the Brexit vote: it was based in the UK, but was heavily dependent on sales in mainland Europe and the fall in the pound sterling against the euro had decimated profits.

His ageing mother continued to be a major drain on his resources, her lack of medical insurance, and dogged insistence on being treated privately, having proved especially punitive recently. He could not afford to buy a house to live in, nor could he afford more than basic monthly maintenance payments to keep Amanda in any style, and certainly not the style to which she aspired. Not a rosy picture, but one which would be presented to the court.

Depressed by their conclusions, the two of them finished their coffees and left the restaurant for a consoling drink in a nearby wine bar.

Once the two men had left, the younger couple in the restaurant compared notes — literally. They had heard every word of the conversation between James and Roger a few tables away, via a powerful directional microphone linked to a mobile phone. They made notes summarising the conversation, which would be presented to their client later that day. They had started their business, F&L Investigations, some two years before and Amanda had been recommended to them. The divorce proceedings had just begun and she wanted to know as much as possible about James; they, as enquiry agents, had been happy to oblige.

Chapter Fourteen
John and Cathy

Leo was back in the restaurant for Monday lunchtime, and the call he was expecting from John Prowse came shortly after midday: "Leo. Great news! The couple who want our house have upped their offer, and we've accepted it! Can I book our usual table for tonight, to celebrate?" Leo was happy to take the booking and was pleased by the turn of events.

What John and Cathy did not know, at least for now, was how the increased offer had come about.

Leo had not been idle the previous Friday and over the weekend. He had spoken at some length to another resident of the mews where John and Cathy lived, in fact to the man who ran the informal residents' association who was a regular at Messanto. They had met later in the day and had then set up a gathering of other residents in the mews. Everyone had attended and there was an air of expectation in the room as they all settled down.

Leo had begun the discussion by saying "You've been kind enough to allow me to join you today, even though I don't live in the mews; but I have met most of you before, in the restaurant." Nods of approval greeted this and Leo pressed on. "John and Cathy have a real dilemma and, unless we talk it through and find an answer, you will all be faced with a dilemma as well. I can bring an outsider's view to bear, with a degree of impartiality."

Seeing more nods of approval, Leo came straight to the point. "First and foremost you need to decide whether you want to live on a major building site for months, perhaps a year or more."

"But how can we stop that happening? If they own the house they can do what they want. We'll just have to live with it." This came from the resident pessimist of the mews, renowned for his expertise in making sure nothing ever happened — his default stance required inactivity, preferably on a grand scale — and his glass was permanently half-empty. As an optimist Leo disagreed with him, but silently, holding back the suggestion the pessimist should pour his half-empty glass into a smaller one, instantly providing a glass that would be more than half-full.

"Speaking personally, I for one would hate to be stuck with a building site and all that goes with it, noise, dust and inconvenience mostly. I'm not sure how we stop it though." This view was echoed by others.

"But it's the impact on our day-to-day life in the mews that worries me most." This from a well-known retired actor (surely, he was resting rather than retired, thought Leo) who spent most of the time at his house in the mews writing his memoirs.

"If we all oppose the planning application, we'll have got off on the wrong foot from the start, not good for neighbourly relations," was another shared view. The unspoken fear was that the strong community spirit which existed at the moment, an important part of mews life, would be shattered within a matter of days.

"I'm worried by security guards, they're usually armed, aren't they?" The question was met with silence, no resident being in the arms or security business.

Sensing agreement in the discussion so far, Leo had then moved the conversation on. "You do realise that, if the works go ahead, the value of your houses will be affected? I think they'll go down in value. No one wants to live in a mews plagued by builders, lorries, noise and dust; leaving aside there'll be permanent security guards in the mews. You really need to think about it."

Surprise had showed on some faces at Leo's view. One resident in particular had though it necessary to play the Devil's Advocate. "I hesitate to disagree with you, Leo," Leo smiled inwardly at this, knowing very well this particular individual spent most of his waking hours finding fault with others, "but I feel it incumbent on me to present the contrary view, even if unconvinced of its merits." Leo suspected he must be a lawyer, although probably not an advocate, but kept his suspicions to himself. "I think you're exaggerating the risks and trying too hard to scare us."

"I gain nothing by scaring you. You're the ones who stand to lose if you're not even a little frightened by what might happen."

"But Leo, if you're right, what can we do about it?"

Leo had anticipated the question. "What can you do? There's no point in speaking to the African buyers, they won't change their minds about the building works. John and Cathy want to move, you can't stop that. Their English buyers can't afford to increase their offer. The sticking point is the sale price. There *is* something you can do, and I think it'll work."

Encouraged by a rapt audience, Leo had outlined his plan. "It comes down to money. You should all act together. If you do, it'll be affordable and will solve the problem. John and Cathy have received two offers, one higher than the other. You should all club together to make good the difference between the two offers, so that the English couple can go ahead but at the price offered by the Africans. That's a comparatively small amount of money each, but well worth it."

Leo had listened as the residents debated the issues and was delighted that, with only a little further prompting from him, they had come to the conclusion (some more rapidly than others) that they would adopt his plan. Leo's solution was sensible and workable. Everyone in the mews would contribute. Leo's powers of persuasion had won the day, without the need to remind anyone that the formal role of Devil's Advocate — the cardinal appointed by the Church to put the view against elevating someone to Sainthood — had been abolished at least thirty years before.

Leo's plan, born of his experience in the property world, had been brought to fruition. He had cleared the basic legalities of this in his conversation with Clive at the restaurant last Thursday evening. Clive, as a practical lawyer, had said it would work (subject to some safeguards, but Leo was familiar with lawyers hedging bets in that way). On learning during Monday morning of the weekend's developments, Clive had discussed the new arrangement with his clients. The increased offer had been made to John and Cathy and had been accepted.

There were details to be sorted out, but the key was that John and Cathy had then been able to make an offer for the Sussex house, which had in turn been accepted. He would also be telling the bank tomorrow that he would be accepting their offer. A celebration was in order, and John had put the call into Leo, booking their usual table for that evening.

Chapter Fifteen
James and Amanda

Later that week, on the Thursday, Elizabeth was working out in her own mind how best to break the news to her client James about the court hearing the following day, when financial aspects of the divorce were due to be aired, argued over, but then adjourned to a later date if Amanda acted true to her previous form. Amanda's lawyer had called unexpectedly to say he would be putting forward a proposal, in the hope that agreement could be reached and the proceedings brought to a conclusion. The proposal had arrived by email an hour later and, to Elizabeth's great surprise, it was a sensible proposal. She felt sure James, even at his most mulish, could be persuaded to accept it with one or two minor tweaks.

Elizabeth, instinctively suspicious of an outbreak of peace in such a highly contentious atmosphere, wondered what had caused Amanda's change of heart. Amanda had chosen her lawyer deliberately, as a man with a reputation for adopting a stance in divorce negotiations about as constructive as King Herod's attitude to childcare in biblical times. On the other hand, bringing such unpleasant proceedings to an end had the advantage for all involved of bringing the stress and strain of constant argument to an end as well: the parties could get on with their lives.

Elizabeth had then called James and told him what had happened. She talked him through the proposal. James shared her suspicions but he agreed (after the compulsory, but on this occasion token, fight) that, at face value, it was a proposal he could accept with the tweaks Elizabeth was suggesting. His financial obligations to Amanda from now on would be less onerous than feared and would not be open-ended. They were to be limited in time, and there would then be a clean break, so that neither of them could come back later and make a claim against the other.

Elizabeth agreed to go back to Amanda's lawyer to put the deal together and if that worked, there would be no need for James to be at court the following day.

***

Roger was sitting in his flat with James as the call from Elizabeth came in. On finishing the call, James turned to Roger immediately, exclaiming with notes of triumph and relief in his voice, "They've fallen for it! We're about to do a deal to bring it all to an end. At last!"

It had been Roger's strategy which had brought it about. He had remained on the fringe of Amanda's circle of friends, James having been ostracised by her with a speed worthy of a gold medal. Amanda's main confidante was a woman with an addiction to gossip, whose way of keeping a secret was to tell no more than two people about it. Any juicy tit-bit told to her would be certain to reach Amanda, and Roger had fed the confidante stories from time to time over the years with this in mind. In return, the confidante had swapped gossip with him, and it was in one such conversation that he had learned, "In confidence of course and, please don't tell a soul," that Amanda was using F&L Investigations. He had paid his dues in return by revealing, in confidence, that James's finances were precarious and that the two of them often discussed his divorce over lunch.

Having fed this into the gossip network, it was only a matter of time before F&L had appeared at Messanto's. Roger and James had agreed their lunchtime script beforehand — it was a mix of the truth, the whole truth and something but the truth.

It was correct to say that the family business was suffering, but hedging had reduced the currency losses. James, a major force as sales director when fully engaged, had taken both feet off the pedals as his marriage collapsed. He had concentrated all his efforts on negotiating two sizeable deals with US-based companies, both of which he would be able to sign up within six months. They would transform the company's finances, but they wouldn't appear in the public accounts for ages yet.

It was true that the medical team on which James's mother relied had an ability to charge amounts of bank-breaking proportions, but James had taken on responsibility for the cost, having agreed with his mother that she would reimburse him at some time in the future once stock markets had recovered.

It was also true that James's relationship with the other woman seemed to have cooled to nearer freezer than fridge level, but this was because she had committed to a two-year academic post in the USA, which would keep her out of harm's (and Amanda's) way for some time yet. They planned to spend time together when James was in the USA putting the new deals together.

James was relieved the pressure was over — he could get on with his life. Roger was also pleased, but mostly because James would be moving out soon. He could then get on with his bachelor life.

***

Amanda's life was changing. She would finally be rid of James, but was she ready for the change which was taking up most of her time?

There had been a certain style attached to James's excesses. If nothing else, James was entertaining and suave. That said, his persistence in getting what he wanted was unpleasant for anyone in his way, but life was never boring when James put his mind to it. James admired his own publicity and, before Amanda, his social media had advertised a bachelor lifestyle given to very few.

Amanda's education had taken her through university as a graduate in media studies, and on to a course at a London school for aspiring actors. She had secured minor roles on tv, but little more, before meeting James. They had married only six months later and the two of them, for a time at least, had enjoyed a period of excess and pleasure; to his mind surfeit was the minimum level to be achieved. Holidays in the Maldives and Mauritius, private yacht charters in the Caribbean, jaunts by private plane to parties in France and sampling the best restaurants the world could offer had all played their part.

The eyewatering expenditure for their lifestyle had been met from a combination of James's family company and, until the wealth had run out, a family trust set up years ago by James's grandfather.

Amanda had been happy to move hedonism to the next level, but her enthusiasm for the consumption overdose had waned as his appetite for it had increased. Their sex life had been sensational at the beginning, but over time James's appetite for other women had also increased, to the extent he made little effort to hide his extra-marital dalliances from her. He had also acquired a degree of fame by appearing in a reality tv show. He had not won, but his opinions and attraction to other contestants had ensured major publicity in social media outlets.

Tests had revealed James was unable to be a father but his reaction had not been one of disappointment, rather he had treated it as an attack on his virility and a licence to seduce as many women as possible.

They had stayed together despite all this, an open marriage (so called) being preferable in Amanda's mind to the alternative of separation and divorce. She had some wealth of her own as well as a healthy allowance from James and could lead a life as separate from James as she wanted. She had indulged herself with the occasional fling — her personal trainer had revitalised her sex life for a while — and her circle of friends were loyal to a fault, only too ready to sympathise with her. To the outside world, James and she had reached an accommodation, but inwardly Amanda knew she could not live her life like this for much longer.

Amanda's life was changed the moment she saw a photo of James on the front page of the *London Evening Standard*, being arrested late the previous night on the way out of a well-known gay club. It also looked like he had started a fight. It was all very well him making a fool of himself — he was a master of that — but allowing his dirty linen to be washed in so public a way was unforgiveable. She had long suspected that his sexual activities did not involve women exclusively, and the report in the paper confirmed this. He would also be lucky to escape an appearance in court on an assault charge.

They had met the next day, but James had refused to accept he was in any way to blame for what had happened or that the publicity was harmful. He had also failed to appreciate — or rather admit — that it would affect Amanda. She should, "Just let it all blow over," he had said, before leaving on a business trip to the USA. The press had been relentless in their efforts to embellish the story, ambushing Amanda outside the house whilst James was away and calling her repeatedly.

Her patience finally exhausted, she had decided to consult a lawyer about a divorce. A friend's recommendation had taken her to a small firm in south-west London, where she had met Mark Hall, a lawyer in his mid-thirties with a reputation for reducing rotweilers to toothless wrecks. His unwritten motto in divorce proceedings — why hit above the belt? — was followed to the letter. His tactics matched Amanda's attitude exactly. They made a good team, frustrating James at every opportunity. James would get his divorce, but only in time and on Amanda's terms.

Away from the law, Mark personally was calm and, in unguarded moments, charming. Amanda was able to look beyond the legal persona he offered to the outside world, and she liked what she saw. The affinity between them had developed as the divorce proceedings had progressed, moving from a dispassionate professional relationship to a passionate affair, which they had both grasped with a special enthusiasm.

Their sexual chemistry had been obvious to them both from the very beginning, but the need to concentrate efforts towards the divorce had delayed the inevitable. They were both in failed marriages but relished the chance to reawaken desires they realised had been on hold for too long. Mark's stamina had surprised Amanda (and Mark) but she was more than receptive to his efforts below the belt. Sexually she felt she was at the perfect stage, between kitten and cougar.

Amanda and Mark also knew that there was more than sex to their lives. Great though life in the bedroom (or kitchen, living room or open air) was, they had found as strong a connection between their minds as their bodies. They had talked about starting a business together which, as the idea took shape, had intrigued them both and had concentrated their minds on the future rather than the past.

Amanda's financial agreement with James in the divorce had been driven as much by the efforts of F&L Investigations as her desire to move on with Mark, both personally and in the new business. She had also realised that it was less fun than before to irritate and frustrate James in the financial negotiations. She was sure he was hiding something from her but cared less about that than before.

She had decided that she must embrace change: it was inevitable and essential. She would move on.

Chapter Sixteen
Owen and Miranda

Owen Lately, self-appointed guru of all things healthy, felt the morning had gone well. He was planning to open a shop in Pimlico, selling health foods, drinks and accessories to a public he was convinced would benefit from a healthier lifestyle. He had just met his accountant to run through the figures and, if all went to plan, the shop would open within two or three months. He had worked singlemindedly in recent years to increase his public profile and was a regular guest on radio and tv when a view was needed on health and lifestyle issues. His podcasts were increasingly popular and his online presence, also increasing, gave him a wider audience, and more quickly, than had been possible even a few years before.

He had no particular qualification to do all this, other than a conviction that his views were right and that, although everyone was free to make a choice, they were making the wrong choice if they disagreed with him. His limited powers of persuasion were coupled with an inability to listen for more than a few seconds — he would then interrupt to air his views, again. He understood the publicity value of a disagreement.

Owen was proud of his family's healthy lifestyle, announced regularly to the public by photo shoots and articles in magazines, coupled with an extensive social media and online presence. If members of the public were unaware of his views on the evils of alcohol and gambling, or the need for healthy eating in an improving lifestyle, it was not for lack of effort on Owen's part. His wife, Miranda, always smiling, supported him at every turn, as did their teenage daughter.

Owen acted as a paid consultant to a number of companies, advising them on attitudes and trends in lifestyle thinking. Although the pay was good, there was something lacking. He did not control the direction his work was taking. His advice helped the companies who paid him but did nothing to help him be recognised as the leading guru in his field: the shop, and the publicity it would attract, would be a major step towards achieving this goal. He also needed to concentrate his efforts. He was going to be more vocal in his opposition to online gambling sites, as well as emphasising the dangers of drink by having cutting-edge interviews with reforming alcoholics. He was devising a coordinated programme of events in support of all this, a reflection of his commitment to improving the lives of others. To the outside world Miranda and he were teetotal, but she had drawn the line at becoming vegetarian as well. He was on his way to Messanto to join Miranda for lunch at their usual table to chat things through over a typically healthy meal. After that he was due to record a radio interview for broadcast later.

He saw the steps he was taking as a natural consequence of his hard work over the years. Outside observers, on the other hand, might see an obsessive personality desperate for a limelight brighter than achieved by winners on Oscar night. Owen knew it was possible to hide his light under a bushel, but in truth he wanted to dispense with the bushel entirely.

***

Miranda was seated at the usual table, waiting for Owen. She had spent a pleasant morning preparing for her Committee Meeting later that afternoon but knew she would need to suffer her husband's views for a couple of hours beforehand. Her patience with Owen was wearing thin these days.

When they had first met as students, she had been as enthusiastic as him about making the world a better place. Direct and indirect aid, properly organised, was essential, as was improved diet and healthcare in developing countries. His geography degree had armed him with a wealth of knowledge few were able to contradict, even if he occasionally over-egged the aid pudding. His enthusiasm was infectious and, on graduating, they had worked as volunteers in various third-world countries to see at first-hand what was needed.

They had married on their return and had both joined high profile charities involved in the aid sector. Miranda had realised that good motives alone were not enough in the charity world, with good management being as important as helping the needy. Her co-workers dealt with aid on the ground, whilst her role ensured that finance and people would be in the right place at the right time. Her financial oversight and command of the logistics required for the charity business were renowned.

It was after a couple of years that Miranda had sensed a change in Owen. At the beginning he had been content to watch and learn, but this had given way to a desire for public recognition of his good work. He wanted to tell the outside world what he had achieved, but more often than not he failed to recognise the contribution of others. His reluctance to accept the views of others unless identical to his was also a problem. Cooperation with others was a reducing part of his armoury, if it could be traced at all, and he was not given to self-criticism. All these factors conspired to make him unemployable in the charity sector, his reputation preceding him too often. Running out of alternatives, he had formed a consultancy (of one person) and had offered his services to organisations, some less than charitable, which had allowed him full rein to operate in areas of his choice with little interference from anyone else.

Miranda had watched Owen move from enthusiasm to obsession. Owen's reputation had continued to grow, not necessarily for the better, but was higher outside the charity sector than within it. He trod on fewer toes when recounting successes than when taking part in them himself. He had embraced a wider agenda, having recognised that a healthier life and lifestyle were becoming increasingly important in the minds of the public. Where Miranda and he parted company was his insistence that the family adhere to the strictest principles — giving up alcohol except for the occasional glass at celebrations and becoming as near vegetarian as possible being only two aspects of many. His liking for different, but to her mind bland, teas was as close as Miranda could come to his way of thinking.

Miranda's dislike of Owen's self-righteous approach had grown in direct proportion to the strength of his opinions. As a family their diet had always been healthy and so she saw no reason to change it fundamentally. Owen's assumption of the moral high ground was as close to forming a new religion as he could get, with Owen as the Saviour. Miranda's resentment of his evangelism grew to the extent that, had she been religious, it would have warranted a confession.

All the same, Miranda realised that to undermine Owen in public would be counterproductive. Getting her own back took more subtle forms. She had become friendly with people in the charity world who had suffered under Owen's fervour, and who were as reluctant as she to adopt his rules. His evangelism struck all the wrong chords with them. They met at regular intervals and the Committee Meeting, to be held in Messanto's private room, was one such occasion.

She looked up and smiled as Owen joined her at the table. "Hello," she said "How was the morning? Were the accountants helpful?"

His reply was typical of him. "I've got to leave for the radio interview in an hour. Let's get the lunchtime menu and order."

She handed him the menu which was already on the table. "Oh, okay," he murmured, adding after a cursory glance at the choices, "I think I'll have a quick bowl of pasta."

Julia was ready to take their order, Miranda having already decided on a salad. They also ordered their usual teas to accompany the meal, a delicate mint infusion for him, tea with lemon for her, served in individual pots and fine china cups. Their choices made and with her mind in neutral, she settled down to listen to Owen's latest sermon on his chosen text for the day.

"You won't believe how the gambling companies behave. They fleece everyone and pay no tax. It's iniquitous. From now on I'm going to make life as difficult as possible for them." Miranda had heard his views on the subject many times before but she avoided saying so by taking a sip of tea. "They should be taxed out of existence and that's just what I'll be saying in the radio interview. There are so many ways to get back at them. The tax authorities just don't know where to begin". Miranda thought his views on the topic would be a cure for insomnia for most listeners but rather than make a comment she took another sip of tea.

By the time they had finished their meal, Owen had voiced his opinions on a number of other subjects, such as the stock he needed for the new shop and how some teas were so much more popular than others. Miranda had offered the occasional comment but might as well have been reading out the shipping forecast for all the attention Owen paid her.

His monologue over, he had left the restaurant, giving her a peck on the cheek and saying, "I might be home later than usual. I'm sure the interviewer will want more than the hour that's in our diaries." Her unspoken reaction to this was to feel a pang of sympathy for the interviewer.

Miranda asked Leo for another pot of tea, to be served in the private room to which she would move in preparation for the Committee Meeting. She had a little more work to do before the Meeting.

***

"Thank you so much for organising this Miranda. We really enjoy ourselves."

This was one of many compliments paid to her by the guests in the private room as they arrived. Ten of them were gathered there and all of them, at one time or another, had worked with Miranda on charitable projects. They all respected her knowledge and skills, seeing the Committee Meetings as an ideal forum in which to exchange views and news. They discussed the problems faced by the charitable sector and, perhaps uniquely amongst forums of this kind, came up with actual suggestions about how to improve what they were doing. They all knew how easy it is to criticise, but how difficult it is to come up with workable solutions.

All the guests had also, at one time or another, run into Owen and had been irritated by his self-promotion and evangelism. There was no competition between the guests, except when sharing tales of how Owen's efforts had been more of a hindrance than a help.

There was also another factor which bound them all together, born from the rise of the self-appointed experts, of whom Owen was a prime example, on how people should run their lives and, no less worrying, how the world at large should behave. These experts were dipping into the charity sector with suggestions, some more helpful than others. The spread of the internet, and the ease with which views of every kind could reach a huge audience, simply made the problem worse.

The erosion of choice, by ridiculing existing methods in favour of untried theories and treating people as the enemy if they disagreed, added to the unease felt by the guests about the way the wind was blowing.

Their presence at the Committee Meetings in Messanto's private room was a way of pushing back the tide. They were able to have sensible discussions with well-informed colleagues, but were also able to relax in private surroundings in a way they rarely encountered in their professional lives. Each guest suffered from one theory or another: alcohol was not allowed unless served in thimbles, meat was permissible only when there was a 'q' in the month, or gambling was evil even when conducted with worthless plastic chips. The ability to let off steam at such restraints had assumed an importance which Miranda had recognised. She had done something about it, and the regular Committee Meetings had begun.

The challenge for the members of the Committee — all the guests — was to fit as much forbidden fruit into the afternoon as time allowed. Miranda had started the ball rolling by ensuring that, whenever she had tea with lemon, it was in fact gin and tonic served with a slice of lemon in a fine china cup. She had adopted this ruse as soon as she had realised Owen would insist on tea with his meals. Rather than waste time arguing with him, it had seemed more sensible to meet the problem head on and for her to have a separate supply of tea with lemon. Other guests had followed her lead and, as a symbol of unity, had asked Leo to supply pots of tea with lemon to those who wanted at the Committee Meetings. He was only too happy to oblige and had already provided a regular supply to Miranda at lunch that day.

Leo, ably assisted by Julia, also served plates of delicious Italian salami and ham, together with mouth-watering cheeses, adding glasses of wine for those who preferred it, or wanted to move on from tea with lemon. For the guests, it was not so much a rebellion — that was too strong a word — as an escape from needless restrictions, free from the gaze of the disapproving health-police and poison of social media.

The most popular item on the agenda for Committee Meetings was different again but brought out a hidden enthusiasm in the members. Miranda ensured that Meetings coincided with race meetings. She had long been a fan of horseracing, along with a small flutter, but Owen's world frowned on such pastimes. The tv in the private room, built into the wall and usually hidden behind a moveable screen, was tuned to whichever channel was showing the races and Miranda acted as an informal bookmaker. She had opened an online account with a major gambling company and put on bets once the guests had decided which horses to back. She kept a book and accounted to everyone after each Meeting, with celebratory pots of tea with lemon on offer to the winners on the day.

The Committee Meetings usually lasted for a couple of hours, sometimes more. Leo was the excellent host and the soul of discretion, telling the world outside that Messanto had hosted a discussion forum on sensitive matters behind closed doors. His note in the restaurant's booking system was that the TWL Charity Committee Members were guaranteed the room for the afternoon. His mental note as the guests departed was to replenish the restaurant's stocks of gin.

Chapter Seventeen
Peter

A week had passed since the lunch at Messanto when the bad news about the Hecht family's finances had been laid so bare. The lunch had been disastrous from Peter Hecht's point of view, as yet another nail in his financial coffin. To receive so much less than expected from his father was part of the problem, but by no means the most pressing.

Claire and Peter had a strong but old-fashioned marriage, in the sense that Claire had given up her job as a trainee hotel manager at the first sign of pregnancy, with no intention of returning to work, then, now or in the future. Peter was expected to provide for the family and to manage all the finances. Their two children were in their late teens, still very much living at home and still very much likely to remain there until the bank of mum and dad coughed up enough to help them onto the housing ladder. They all lived in a rambling house in Sussex, which required a level of maintenance which had surprised the bank manager when Peter had first asked for a loan to cover roof repair costs. Peter's DIY skills were legendary for their inadequacy, which had forced him to rely on builders who had lost no opportunity to send in bills which resembled the annual aid budget for smaller African countries.

Peter was good at his job, the PR company he worked for being a good employer with good clients, well-suited to a person with Peter's business drive. Peter's salary, and occasional bonus, had kept pace with his expenditure and allowed his head to stay above water, even if his overdraft increased whenever Claire embarked on one of her regular shopping expeditions with the children. It was still a mystery to Peter why every item needed a designer label — to him, shopping was a necessary chore rather than an experience to be enjoyed repeatedly.

A year ago it had all changed. The PR company had failed to carry out sufficiently detailed checks on a new client, a high-profile company with an international presence. To act for a company with this range and scope for the first time had been seen as a positive move in the market at the time. Deeper research would have revealed the unacceptable face of its operations, exploiting children abroad to manufacture its goods and with a board of directors more skilled in crime than altruism. Bad news travels the fastest, and before Peter's company could mount a counteroffensive the damage had been done: the PR company had lost clients as a result and it would be a while before the business could be won back, if it could be won back at all.

A restructuring of the business had been inevitable, with certain employees being made redundant and others, including Peter, put on a part-time basis on a much-reduced salary. As from six months ago, he had been paid half the salary to work half the time he had worked before. Peter had considered whether to change jobs but, according to the head-hunters he had visited, the market was difficult for people of his age and experience. He was also associated with the disaster, even if he had played no part in it.

He had not yet told Claire and the children about it. Apart from his wounded pride, he wasn't sure he could face Claire's disappointment in him, or her impatience to solve the problem. He still travelled up to London every day, maintaining the façade of being fully employed. His loyalty cards with coffee shops were extensive, but his capacity for coffee was reaching saturation point. He had read more indifferent novels and visited more art galleries in the last few months than he would ever admit. He was sure the position would right itself given time, but time was running out, as was his credit with the bank and credit card companies. The house was mortgaged to the hilt. His and Claire's cars were leased, not owned. His overdraft was at its limit. His savings had vanished after the latest house repairs and he had been relying on money coming from his father's estate to pay off at least some of the mounting debts. The financial façade he had built over the years was crumbling, but so far without it becoming public knowledge.

Peter's pride was hurt, but he would not admit it to anyone. How could he turn it all round without anyone finding out how dire his position was? He could not admit failure to anyone, and certainly not to his wife or mother, nor to his brother, Graham, whose infuriating response to all problems was "something will turn up". At this rate bailiffs would be the first to turn up unless he found a solution.

***

Walter Hecht had been not only an astute businessman, but a skilled art collector as well. His skill had been in finding promising artists before their rise to fame. His interest in art had been kindled during his youth, which he had spent in his native Germany before the rise of the National Party and the Hitler Youth movement had forced his parents to leave for England, where Walter's cousins already lived. He had built up a small but carefully chosen collection of paintings by lesser-known European artists, waiting for public taste to catch up with him. His occasional failures were more than outnumbered by his successes, his faith in public taste veering from the lowest point possible (was it really necessary to explain that Moby Dick wasn't a seventies porn movie?) to a higher level where public taste approached his.

Walter had acquired some paintings — the most speculative in terms of when values might increase —

and had immediately put them in the names of his children. A few days ago Peter had taken one of these paintings to a well-known art dealership in the West End for an evaluation. The painting was from the Pre-Raphaelite school, bought for a song in the 1960s by Walter and then passed on to Peter at the earliest opportunity. The painting was not by one of the leading artists of the time but had been well chosen. The expert at the dealership had salivated over the painting, assuring Peter of its authenticity and marketability.

Peter had thanked the expert for her time, promising to return soon with the painting to discuss how best to sell it. If it achieved the value suggested by the expert his financial worries would be hugely reduced, down to a manageable level.

A plan to sort it all out had formed in his mind, but the problem was Claire. She was no art expert, but always drew attention to the painting when visitors came to the house. It had pride of place in the living room, carefully hung with discreet lighting to show it to best effect. She would never agree to it being sold — in her eyes it was a special attraction in the house, and she was right. How then might Peter realise its value without Claire knowing?

The answer had come to him after reading an article in the Sunday papers about the art world and the dangers encountered by collectors. Fraud was playing an increasing role in the market. It had always fascinated Peter that, by definition, the best forgery had not been discovered. He had told Claire that he was taking the painting to a specialist restorer to assess its condition. Should it be restored or cleaned, for example? In reality he was on his way to an artist's studio in Islington with a completely different purpose in mind.

Peter knew that insurance premiums for valuable works of art were heavy to say the least, and the latest premium for the painting had done nothing to lower his blood pressure. According to the article there was a growing practice for copies of artworks to be made and then put on display, with the original being kept in a safe place. This saved massively on insurance premiums, but Peter had a broader plan. He was on his way to see an artist whose reputation had been founded on forgery but who, once he had been released from prison, had applied his skills in a different way. He was intrigued to meet the artist whose livelihood depended on legitimate deception.

Peter's plan was to commission the artist to make an exact copy of the painting, using a canvas and materials consistent with the age of the painting. The artist's reputation for quality preceded him, and his work would survive all but the most careful professional scrutiny. The copy would be placed in the original frame and hung on the wall at home.

He would then be free to sell the original painting.

To Claire, art was useful decoration but little more. Peter had once referred to pictures being of museum quality, provoking the tart response that he was the only object she knew of that quality. Her passion was to find obscure designers of curtains and fabrics, and she would then concentrate on being solely responsible for keeping them in business. The same applied to furniture designers she found. Housing magazines were in no rush to feature her efforts, but everyone agreed her choices provided interesting, even unique, results.

Claire had shown little interest in new acquisitions in the art market. Her one rule was to insist that she must be able to recognise instantly whether a picture was the right way up, an attribute not always obvious with some of the more modern artists. She would be none the wiser when the picture was back safely on the living room wall and, when that had been done, he would be free to sell the original. This could not be at auction, which would attract unwelcome publicity and he chose to ignore Claire's likely reaction if his deception were to come to light. Their relationship had survived the odd challenge in the past, but to Peter the combination of problems he faced today was not something to be shared with Claire, but something out of the ordinary, threatening the very blocks on which their life was built and which he alone would overcome.

His visit to another lawyer to see if he could sue Anthony had come to nothing. The lawyer had sympathised, but advised that Walter had been free to make his own decisions. The cost of suing would have been prohibitive, apart from the uncertainties of litigation. Peter had left the meeting with the impression it would be more productive for him to put a large sum on the second-favourite in the Derby than sue Anthony.

The specialist dealer had assured him a private sale could be achieved with no publicity attached. Her suggested commission on the sale had stopped just short of jeopardising his health, but in the turmoil of his finances looked well worthwhile. He would go ahead with the sale.

It had not occurred to Peter that Claire was more understanding and perceptive than he realised. She knew her husband was in financial difficulty. In recent months he had moved to be nearer Scrooge than Croesus. She also sensed that his office was taking up less time than before. But his pride — selfish to her mind — was untouchable. She was impatient to help him but kept it in check. For now, so soon after his father's death, she had no desire to upset the applecart (although there was no guarantee she would recognise one of those unless it had a designer label), and devoted her efforts to the children, whose need for attention, not to say independence, was growing by the day. She was not afraid of confrontation, but you could measure Peter's reaction to it on the Richter Scale. She would choose her moment — and ammunition.

Meanwhile, Peter persisted in juggling with the various façades in his life.

Chapter Eighteen
Graham

Graham Hecht was on his way to Messanto, to join Amanda and Mark. He had met them only once before, for a few minutes over coffee, when they had recruited him as a client of their new business. The three of them were to meet over a supper that evening, so that they could chat in a relaxed but more concentrated way.

Manmar Consultants Ltd., Amanda and Mark's new business, specialised in helping people such as Graham by introducing them to like-minded individuals at a level not available from online, bulk-dating services. Mark's work as a divorce lawyer depended on broken relationships but would provide a ready stream of clients for Manmar Consultants. Amanda's circle of friends would be fertile ground for clients as well.

Amanda and Mark would help clients to forge new relationships, usually after the wreckage of divorce. Both of them well understood how tempting it was, even after the divorce battles and financial fighting were long gone, to resurrect the bitterness every now and again. It was surely better to concentrate on the future than dwell on the past.

His father's recent death had caused Graham to take stock of his life. His antiques business was a success, but without being spectacular. He had inherited the artistic side of his father's nature, but without the drive needed for real business success. If he was marking time in his business life, the same could be said of his personal life, where his reluctance to commit for longer than a few months at most had caused a couple of promising relationships to dissolve into recrimination and flying crockery.

Graham's reluctance to commit was deep-seated, not fixed by the character traits he had inherited from his parents. As Graham walked through the streets of Pimlico, he recalled a time when he was in his mid-twenties, working as a junior in one of the London auction houses to learn about the antiques business. He was sharing a flat in Fulham with friends at the time and had been going out with a girl for several months. She was special to him and he made every effort to show her how special she was — a number of his earlier dates with girls had fallen foul of a natural diffidence he was too naïve to hide — and their relationship was going from strength to strength.

At the same time, Graham's mother was trying hard to see if her two sons could bury whatever hatchets were between them. To her, blood was infinitely thicker than water and she felt they would come to regret a rift so deep it could never be healed. She was constantly at them to get together and, if not just the two of them, then with other people there as well. Her persistence paid off and they agreed to meet for a meal one evening at Peter's flat, bringing their girlfriends with them.

Peter was already making a name for himself in the PR business, but even the basic charm he employed at work was noticeable by its absence that evening. His self-imposed rivalry with his brother surfaced in several ways, not the least of which was to ignore Graham as far as was humanly possible, whilst denigrating the art world and emphasising his growing success in the PR world. Peter was a passable host to everyone but Graham that evening, and on the way home Graham and his girlfriend had joked that Peter should at least go to charm school, even if he would probably fail whatever tests were set.

For the first serious time in his life, and to his surprise, Graham displayed a firmness of purpose, triggered by the evening with his brother. He bought an engagement ring with his savings and set up an evening for the following Saturday to propose — the restaurant was primed to serve champagne if she said yes. The scene was set.

His plan unravelled in spectacular fashion when she called him on the Friday to say she needed some space and they should not meet for a while. "It's not you, it's me," she said. Graham's blood ran cold at that moment, suspecting the opposite was true and he was the cause. Nothing he said convinced her to change her mind, and they had parted as friends.

Peter called him a couple of months later, out of the blue, to announce he and Claire were engaged and that she had certainly chosen the right brother.

Peter was not seeking Graham's congratulations: his call had been motivated by spite, to rub his brother's nose in the victory. Graham's dislike for his brother had turned into a deep loathing at that moment, never to recover. If he ever saw his brother again it would be too soon.

His feelings for Claire had never diminished over the years. He had attended his brother's wedding out of love for Claire, but had seen them only rarely since. His mother, knowing a brick wall when she saw one, stepped back in the hope that Graham would find someone else, a hope that had proved forlorn.

He still had the engagement ring, locked away at home. He just couldn't bring himself to part with it.

***

Amanda and Mark were sitting at what they hoped would become their usual table at Messanto. It was at the rear of the restaurant, a corner table for two when romance was in the air but comfortably large enough to allow a third diner to be seated as well. Graham Hecht was due to join them in a few minutes, as a client of Manmar Consultants — Leo, attentive as ever, had been instrumental in introducing Graham to them — and they were chatting through the possibilities for him.

In a brief chat a few days before, Graham had mentioned a failed relationship in the past and his reluctance to commit, but with no details. He clearly was not someone to rush into decisions, but if Aesop's tortoise was anything to go by, his chosen speed might win the day given enough encouragement and sleeping hares. He had also described his antiques business and what it entailed. Graham had not revealed how long it had been since his last relationship, but the two of them agreed that Graham must concentrate on the future: they had already identified someone for him to meet as part of this process, much the same age as him and with similar interests.

The conversation over dinner with Graham that evening flowed, as did the wine. Graham's likeable personality shone through, fuelled as much by the Valpolicella Ripasso as by careful prompts from Amanda and Mark. They were reassured, although Graham's reluctance to reveal much about his close relatives made him an honorary member of the clam family.

Graham had left the restaurant in a much more optimistic frame of mind than he had expected, thanking his hosts for their hospitality and armed with the contact details of the person they suggested he should meet. She worked in the antiques business. Her name was Caroline. He would call her in the morning.

Chapter Nineteen
Caroline

Caroline was waiting for Graham in an upmarket coffee shop in the West End, close to the gallery where she worked. Upmarket was no exaggeration, given the prices of the patisserie on display and a calorie count to test even the most hardened glutton. She had chosen a table facing the door rather than the lines of cream and chocolate-covered pastry.

Graham had suggested the venue in his call to her the previous day, a call she had been expecting after a chat with Amanda. Despite an outward confidence, deployed to great effect in her working life, Caroline felt a few butterflies at work in her stomach at the thought of meeting Graham that morning; not because of him particularly, but because a failed marriage had left her nervous of another relationship. After the divorce, her devotion to work had proved no substitute for a social life, and encouraged by her friend Amanda, "You'll never forgive yourself if you carry on like this," she had resolved to find her life again, even if it meant kissing a few frogs on the way.

Amanda's description of Caroline — petite, dressed by designers, broad smile, stylish blonde hair cut short and she'll be having an expresso, not an éclair — enabled Graham to spot Caroline straight away. He ordered an expresso for himself, and another for her, and the ice was broken quickly when they agreed to ignore all calories on offer. Manmar recommended that a first meeting should be over coffee, rather than a full meal. That allowed a quick exit if all went badly from the outset. There was no such problem for Graham and Caroline for whom the time raced by.

Their conversation covered everything except their past relationships — admissions of failure were for another day. Both had been advised by Manmar to think of the future, an easy task for them because they both worked in the antiques business and shared an enthusiasm for it. They discussed their respective roles, and found common ground in a liking for late nineteenth and early twentieth century art. They were both directors of their businesses, and both were looking for new avenues to follow to broaden their business horizons.

They agreed to meet the following morning at Caroline's gallery — she said she would value his view of a painting a client was bringing to the gallery and Graham was delighted to help — before moving on to Messanto for lunch. He would book the table.

***

The following morning, Caroline was waiting at the gallery where she worked. The client, Mr Hall, was due in a few minutes. He had visited her once before to get a preliminary view, and they were now going to discuss what restoration or cleaning should be undertaken before the painting was put on the market for sale. Hundreds of pounds well spent now could add thousands to the sale price, and she would organise whatever work was needed. Mr Hall had agreed to leave the painting with her after the meeting today. Graham's knowledge would be invaluable to her, not to say the client as well, but Graham wasn't able to join her for another hour or more, by which time Mr Hall would have left.

She was looking forward to seeing Graham, both for his professional views and the pleasure of his company. Coffee with him yesterday had proved a more enjoyable experience than she had anticipated, all trace of her butterflies having disappeared by the second expresso. He was knowledgeable on many subjects, but mainly the art world that fascinated — and fed — them both. He had a relaxed attitude but warmed up noticeably when a subject (or his partner in conversation she wondered?) interested him.

She thought his ideas on how to keep his business, and hers, ahead of the game were well worth another conversation. He had caught her hint before it had dropped too far by inviting her to lunch today at Messanto. She had seen Mr Hall as planned and was collecting her thoughts when Graham joined her a few minutes later. She greeted him with her warmest smile, and after his gratifying smile in return, began her report on the discussion with Mr Hall. "That went well. He wants to sell quickly but knows he needs to spend something to get the best price."

The painting was on the table, loosely wrapped for protection, and she unwrapped it so that Graham could look at it properly. The shock on his face caused Caroline to take a step back, startled by the intensity of his reaction. She had no way of knowing that the picture was none other than the Pre-Raphaelite picture so prized by his brother and Claire. Graham recognised it instantly, Peter never losing the opportunity to refer to it pointedly on Graham's rare visits to the house.

Graham's shock gave way to indignation. What was Peter up to? What was he hiding? Did Claire know about it? Why sell one of the family jewels? He would make it his business to find out. He told Caroline he would join her at the restaurant later because something urgent had come up. Her instincts told her to ask no questions as he brushed past her and out into the street.

***

Peter was uncomfortable with subterfuge, and not very good at it. Desperate for secrecy about the sale, it had not occurred to him that his name might also be made public. He had realised it, late in the day, when asked by

Caroline for his name when he had called to arrange his first visit to the gallery. Surprised by her request but unwilling to give his true name, he had looked round the room for inspiration and his gaze had alighted on a programme for the Promenade Concerts in London. "My name's Albert Hall" he had said. He was now stuck with it, although the name had provoked more amusement than ridicule at the gallery. How could his parents have saddled him with a name like that?

And so it was that, as Mr Hall, he was dealing with the gallery, the restorers and the artist making the copy. He had just left the painting at the gallery, having agreed what restoration and cleaning was needed to make it even more saleable than it already was. Caroline would organise everything for him, and with his secret intact he could concentrate on other things.

On leaving the gallery he had called to confirm his interview in a few minutes with another head-hunter, who wanted to talk him through 'a possible job opportunity'. His optimism on that front was in short supply, but he could not afford to ignore even a slim chance of success in his search.

Peter was unaware that his strategy was in danger. Graham was intent on undermining him and was working out how best to do it.

Subconsciously, Graham was dwelling on the past and couldn't see how destructive his obsession with his brother had become.

***

Caroline arrived at Messanto before Graham and so had time to reflect on the morning's events. Graham had obviously recognised Mr Hall's picture, but his reaction had been so exaggerated that she knew other forces were at work. Graham owed her an explanation if only out of common courtesy but, that said, she would wait for Graham to broach the subject. She sensed he would resent too inquisitive an approach from her and didn't want to spoil her first lunch with him.

Graham joined Caroline at his usual table. She only realised there was such a thing when Leo showed him to 'your usual table Mr Hecht'.

Graham's apology was immediate, if incomplete. "I'm so sorry about what happened. Please forgive me. Let's order and I'll tell you all about it." Her eyebrow was raised in a lower arch than might have been justified, but she smiled in agreement as they turned their attention to the menu.

Chapter Twenty
Walter

Anthony was preparing for another difficult session with the Hecht family. Walter's will had been clear about several things, the first of which Anthony had already revealed — the unwelcome dearth of cash — but Walter wasn't finished with his family. As a result, nor was Anthony. There was another clause in the will, a 'wake clause'. Walter had provided funds to pay for dinner one evening in the private room at Messanto, the guests for the occasion to be Anthony plus certain named members of the family. Walter's funeral was the day after tomorrow, and the wake was scheduled for this evening; the guests were due in a few minutes.

Walter had left instructions about the evening, but in a sealed envelope to be opened after his death. On opening the envelope, Anthony found Walter had been particularly precise in his demands, stipulating not only who the eight guests should be but also where they should sit at the table. Henrietta, Peter and Graham were all invited and Graham was to bring a partner. He had nominated Caroline, a new arrival on the scene for the family. Anthony secretly admired her courage in accepting the invitation to an evening which promised more attrition than sensitivity. Claire had accepted the invitation, any reluctance on her part vanishing when she realised the guest list included Walter's estranged wife, Natasha and daughter, Anne.

Most curiously of all, Walter had provided a present for each guest, box-shaped and wrapped in identical paper with gift tags on them. All the presents were of identical size, on the table beside each place card. Walter had wrapped the presents and his instructions were typically clear — on no account should they be opened until the evening at Messanto. Henrietta had no idea of Walter's plans for the evening. She was not surprised that Natasha and Anne were included, but found it strange that the evening would be the first occasion when the family, apart from her, had met either of them.

Anthony was in the private room with Leo, finalising the arrangements. Walter had chosen the wines — Anthony was not to know that Walter had consulted Leo and Julia at some length about the right food and drink for the evening — stipulating that the finest Italian sparkling wine, not Prosecco but from Lombardy, should be served as the guests arrived. His choice was well-made and the guests showed no reluctance to sample it. They had all arrived within a few minutes of each other, sharing a sense of uncertainty, if not unease, about the form the evening would take. They knew Walter had set up the whole event, but why he had done it remained a mystery to them. None of Walter's friends were present, it was for family, plus Anthony, who was almost part of the family given the length of time he had been involved.

Henrietta took charge of welcoming the guests, so that Natasha and Anne, as new faces, were made to feel welcome from the very first glass. Caroline was also a new face, but well able to cope with probing (to put it politely in Claire's case) questions about herself. Caroline had agreed with Graham not to mention Mr Hall's existence to the room, and Peter was shocked to see Caroline, he had no idea she knew Graham. He made a huge effort to hide his reaction and avoided her as much as the confines of the room allowed.

The conversation in the room didn't flag, although Peter and Graham ignored one another as far as possible. Guests put their differences aside; hostilities were parked and peace prevailed, with curiosity replacing animosity at least for the moment.

The preliminaries over, it fell to Anthony to act as the informal master of ceremonies. Once the assembled company had taken their seats, he revealed Walter's plans for the evening. Walter had paid for everything, drinks included. The meal would have three courses, with a choice of wines. There would be a pause after the second course for reasons which would become apparent. The evening would then move on to a special pudding, followed by coffee and drinks from the bar for those who had the inclination (and stamina). The presents should remain unopened until Anthony gave the word.

His preamble complete, Anthony took his seat at the table with Henrietta on one side of him, Anne the other. He had met Anne only once before, in his office a few days ago to run over legal details with her and her mother. She had matched her father's description of her. "Charming, intelligent and sensitive. As I think about it, more like her mother than her father."

Anthony sat back for a moment, relieved to hear a gentle hubbub of conversation round the table rather than more strident voices. So far, so good. The food, wine and service were excellent, Messanto, Leo and Julia at their best. The presents remained unopened despite obvious temptation. There was a lingering respect for Walter and his wishes, even if he had not always been the easiest of men to deal with.

They had finished the second course when, as Walter had stipulated, a pause was due: this was no random pause, as Anthony revealed. "Walter has left a message for you all. He recorded it a few months ago when he was finalising the details of this evening. He didn't want you to hear it until this stage of the evening, by which time you would all have relaxed a little. I'll play it for you now." He indicated the tv screen on the wall, which sprang into life showing Walter sitting at his desk at home. To say he commanded the room from afar was to understate the effect on his audience. You could hear the sound of pins dropping as Walter, his voice strong, began his message.

"Thank you all for coming. I hope you're enjoying yourselves and I'm sorry I can't be there with you." The deliberate irony of this was not lost on his audience, but they had no time to dwell on it as Walter continued. "I'll come straight to the point, because you'd rather be finishing your meal than listening to me. In the last few months, I've had time to think about my life; a cliché, I know, but please bear with me. My mistakes, at home and in business, have been as frequent as my successes, but it's the mistakes that have caused the greatest damage. If you inherit anything from me, it should be the lessons you learn from my mistakes."

Walter paused on screen, to take a sip of water but also to let the thought sink in. "I can't dictate from the grave, nor do I want to, but I can leave you food for thought. In front of you is a present. You can open it now." Walter sat silently to allow time for this to happen.

As instructed, all eight guests unwrapped their presents. Everyone had four pieces of a chess set. Not a typical set, but made of the finest porcelain, delicate and hand-painted. With one exception, each had two pawns, plus two other pieces such as a bishop or rook. The exception was Anthony, who had both kings and both queens.

Walter's voice filled the room again. "What you have between you is a complete chess set. Each of you has the four pieces I've given you. I bought the set in the late 1960s when such things weren't fashionable," which was Walter's way of saying he had bought at a good price, "and you should know that the set dates from the mid-eighteenth century, made in China and exported to royalty in England, as so often happened all those years ago." Walter continued, in full flow. "The market today is good, but I believe it will get even better in the coming years. The fashion for the wealthy in China is to buy back what was exported, so that their heritage is returned to what they believe is its rightful home." Walter's imposing presence on screen kept his audience mesmerised. "You each have only a small part of the set. Your four pieces on their own are worth perhaps a few thousand pounds each. The greatest value lies in the complete set as a whole. The complete set's value today is in the tens of thousands at least, almost certainly more." Astonished, the guests looked at their presents in a new light.

"And there is one final point to emphasise" added Walter. "I firmly believe that, if you wait, the value of the set will more than double in the next five years."

Walter paused, to add emphasis to his closing words. "I have neglected my relationships with all of you in my lifetime, a major communication failure on my part. I regret that, as you now realise. You all need to decide, together, what you will do with the set. You can only do that by communicating. Consider what you value. Please take the opportunity I am offering you."

As the screen faded away the guests in the room sat silently, each wrapped in their own thoughts, working out what Walter had done and how it affected them. It was as if a slow fuse had been lit on screen, smouldering into the future.

The chess set had been Walter's idea, and his alone. He had talked to Anthony about it for the first time when outlining the arrangements for the wake evening. It now fell to Anthony to deal with the family. Walter had been most insistent that Anthony should take the lead.

"Walter asked me to make a few comments about all this," said Anthony. "Walter hoped you would find time before the funeral to talk amongst yourselves about the conundrum he has left you with." Anthony looked round the room at the inquisitive faces, but no one said a word. He continued. "You each have part of a chess set. Walter stipulated you should all benefit equally from it. The real value of the set, both as a work of art and financially, can be found by you all agreeing to join forces and keeping the set together. You all need to agree what to do. You each have a choice to make. If any one of you chooses not to join in and goes their own way, they will destroy the real value, but for everyone, including themselves.

Anthony himself, was of course, one who needed to make a choice, but he was constrained by a different problem. The rules of his profession prohibited him from benefiting from Walter's estate — he had made this clear to Walter. "I know," had been Walter's terse response. "I see your role as knocking heads together and then stepping aside in whatever way your profession will allow."

As tasks go, thankless didn't begin to describe it. Anthony's judgement calls would need to make even Solomon jealous.

Walter had left one final instruction about the dinner that evening, which Messanto's had followed to the letter. The special pudding was a cake which Leo brought in with a flourish, no ordinary cake, but one the same shape and design as a chess board, with squares marked on it and colouring to match the chess set itself. Each guest was served with a slice, placed alongside their chess pieces. The scene Walter had conjured in his mind was now complete.

The gastronomic side of the evening had concluded according to Walter's instructions. It was now up to the guests to make what they might of the evening's legacy. A cynic might say a game was being played, with the prize of having your cake and eating it too.

Walter had proved much more revealing about himself from beyond the grave than in his lifetime. That in itself was surprising and his message was clear. But to what extent was cooperation possible within the disparate group at the restaurant that evening? They had all agreed that the food and wine had been of the highest quality, but what other common ground existed? Which motivations would prevail?

Anthony sat at the heart of it all, at the centre of the web. Never one to jump to conclusions, a luxury he avoided as a professional, his first thought on learning of the chess set was to ask himself whether Walter was aiming to provoke dissent in the family, or to encourage reconciliation. Walter's tactics in business had avoided the vanilla approach, more often bearing the hallmarks of Machiavelli.

Although a patient man, Anthony was reaching the end of his tether with the family. Disputes and differences left to fester for so long, sometimes decades, were sure to bring disappointment, but the family members were so blind they couldn't see how destructive they were.

Anthony was aware of the conflicting emotions in the family. Walter had drip-fed him nuggets over the years, and he had learned much from the conversations round the table that evening. Without careful handling, tempers would flare, bridges would be burned and all that would remain would be a list of entries for Grudge of the Month.

Anthony would follow Walter's wishes and would encourage discussion within the family. Discussions themselves were often as important at the outcomes and without dialogue, the family might as well step into a boxing ring with no referee. Anthony added his own gloss on this — there was no point in him beginning the discussions unless he knew where they would end. Aimless debate would guarantee failure. He needed to adopt a more radical approach: he had the makings of a plan, which he hoped would work and at least bring the family closer together.

Everyone would reconvene at Messanto in a week's time. By then the funeral would have taken place and everyone would have had a chance to reflect. Also by then Anthony would have been able to take his courage in both hands: he would launch his plan onto the unsuspecting family.

Chapter Twenty-one
Walter

The funeral in the parish church in Sussex a few days ago had proved to be a trial. Walter's estranged wife, Natasha, was technically his widow, but Henrietta had been with Walter for the last thirty years and more. Precedence in the church pews was a problem, resolved by Anthony suggesting that Natasha sit on one side of the aisle with her family, Henrietta and her family on the other. Never had an aisle looked wider, either to the other members of the congregation or to the two families. The service was well attended despite the fact Walter had made as many enemies as friends in his business dealings, and the reception afterwards was marked more by stilted conversation than fond memories of Walter. It was a relief to all concerned when it had ended.

The chess problem preyed on the minds of the family. Solving the problem demanded a balance to be drawn between animosity and profit, a conflict no member of the family was programmed to resolve: the Hecht family's DNA didn't include what was needed. Anthony's lead was vital, and he had been busy in the few days since the funeral. He and the family were now gathered again in the private room at Messanto for an evening when decisions would be taken, if all went according to Anthony's plan.

Henrietta's smile that evening was hiding her memories of Walter's difficult side; she recalled his determined pursuit of Natasha and ruthlessness in ditching her. His pursuit of Henrietta had been equally determined. The wake and funeral had brought the past to life: how Natasha had told her all those years ago, bluntly, that their friendship was at an end because Henrietta had caused the break-up. The two of them had exchanged more Christmas cards than words over the years. She would never be welcome in Natasha's house.

Natasha had refused to introduce Anne to the other side of the family and had also refused to please Henrietta by agreeing to a divorce. Natasha had swallowed her pride, and dislike of Henrietta, to come to London for Walter's funeral. The wake and funeral had proved better than she had expected because more people were there than just close family, but nothing had happened for her to regain any affection for Henrietta. She would not build any bridges with that woman.

Anne was in a strange position and felt curiously detached from the other guests. She had met Walter on his infrequent visits to Nothern Ireland, but the bond between them was not strong. Whether this was because he had always been little more than a visitor in her youth, rather than a doting father, she couldn't decide, but the fact remained they had never been close. If he felt any love for her, it was of the silent kind — he was not a man to wear his heart on his sleeve.

Walter was also set in his ways and suspicious of change, which had made it impossible for him to accept her sexuality. At school and later at college, she had experimented with both boys and girls. She had only established a fulfilling relationship after meeting a nurse, Rosemary, during a spell in hospital for treatment of a kidney infection. They had hit it off straight away and had set up home together in Belfast shortly after.

They were still together, but neither Walter, nor more openly her mother, could accept what had happened. Anne had become estranged from her parents and had come to London more out of interest than any sense of loss. She had no idea how to deal with the chess problem set by Walter. She would watch and wait.

Peter's thoughts were in disarray. He was worried that Graham would reveal his plans to sell the painting, which would infuriate Claire. His wife was well able to find the right choice of insult when put to the challenge. Even worse, his pressing need for money would be revealed, a public disgrace he had to avoid.

Claire couldn't help but notice her husband's discomfort. Peter had never been able to hide his thoughts from her for long. She always got to the root of any problem of his, even if it took time, but she realised there was no point in forcing the issue now, there was more to be gained by waiting. As for the chess set, to her mind any fool could see that the family should come together and sell the set — it was simply a question of when, not if, to sell. Whether the rest of the family would find that logic so compelling was the problem. Graham was likely to be the main fly in the ointment for that, his loathing for his brother had clouded his thinking for so long.

Caroline's first, so far unspoken, thought was that she was surprised to be included as a beneficiary and needed to think carefully about that; but her greater concern was that it would be an artistic crime to split up the chess set. It was an exquisite and rare work of art, and to her it would be vandalism not to keep the pieces together. Value was important, but always going hand-in-hand with artistic integrity. She would press Graham to think that way too, but she was learning that family history had a way of undermining even the most sensible thoughts in the Hecht family.

Graham was vacillating, a skill he had perfected over time. He recognised the value of the set as a whole, but balanced this against the real chance of crushing his brother at last. Peter was clearly in dire straits financially, a realisation that gave Graham unexpected pleasure. Graham had no real need for the money and so could wait and frustrate his brother for as long as it took to extract his pound of flesh, preferably more. He also realised that his ability to reveal Peter's parlous financial state was itself a weapon. By not revealing it, the sword of Damocles remained over Peter's head. It called to mind the old saying: the masochist says 'hit me', the true sadist says 'no'.

Anthony knew that finding a solution would not be a question of asking the family to see reason — compromise would never feature on the family's agenda — but of leaving only one alternative on the table. Anthony needed to transform the art of the impossible into the art of the possible.

**

Justin Altoh, an acknowledged expert on Chinese works of art, with Export Porcelain being a particular interest of his, had arrived at Messanto to meet Anthony and the Hecht family. Justin worked for one of the leading London auction houses. His career had begun in Hong Kong, where he had been born to a Hong Kong-Chinese father and an English mother. He had spent several years living with his parents in Hong Kong and learning the auction business. He had arrived in England ten years ago with his recently widowed mother. His father had ridden his motorcycle once too often at a speed categorised by all insurance companies as terminal. His mother's decision to return to her native England had coincided with an offer from the auction house in Hong Kong for him to work in their London specialist department, an offer Justin had accepted with alacrity.

Justin was now in his late forties and was known for not only his extensive range of contacts but also his knowledge and innovative approach in his chosen field. He had inherited his father's appetite for risk, but happily without the frustration of one who aspired to be a motorcycle racer whilst lacking the requisite skills. He had worked with Anthony before, and had been fascinated by Anthony's description of the Hecht family when the two of them had met a few days ago. He was equally fascinated by the chess set and what might be done with it. He had examined the set and, after research and discussion with his colleagues, was convinced that the set was unique in its rarity, beauty and saleability. Anthony had given him free rein to come up with an approach and Justin would present his ideas to the family.

Leo showed Justin into the private room, where the complete set was laid out on the table as an unsubtle reminder of what had brought them all together that evening. The atmosphere was the wrong side of frosty (arctic was the warmest word for it) as Justin shook hands with everyone and introduced himself. Anthony had warned him in advance not to read too much into the welcome he would receive and so Justin decided to move ahead quickly and outline his thoughts.

"Thank you for inviting me here this evening," he began, despite knowing that the invitation had not been greeted warmly by everyone in the room. "I've spoken to Anthony about the chess set and my role is to come up with a solution. I'm sure Walter was right in saying the greatest value is in the set as a whole, but there is still value, although much lower proportionately, in each individual piece." So far, so obvious, thought Justin, but he pressed on. "What happens if you each keep your own pieces of the set? 'Nothing' is the answer, except that you'll each have attractive pieces to gather dust on some shelf somewhere. You may have personal reasons for deciding to hang on to your pieces, and I won't question them. They are for you individually and have nothing to do with my role here." Justin was looking directly at Graham when saying those words. "But if just one of you refuses to sell, the value of the whole set is lost to everyone. That means the world at large, as well as all of you. No one will be able to see or appreciate the whole as a unique and outstanding work of art. You can see for yourselves the quality of the set" he added, pointing to the table, "and to refuse to sell is a question of conscience for each of you." Justin had felt compelled to bring up questions of conscience, not to say morality, although he suspected the impact would be greater on some of his audience than others.

"It's also true that the set may increase substantially in value over time, but what does that mean? It's not certain to increase in value. It also means waiting for a few years to see if this happens, which assumes you can all agree what to do with the set meanwhile. Who will keep the set and pay the insurance premiums, or will you each keep your own pieces? Is one of you prepared to take on the responsibility of keeping the set? What happens if one of you accidentally damages your pieces? Will you compensate the others for the loss in value to the set?" Justin had agreed with Anthony to stress the problems of waiting for the set to increase in value. The prospect of getting the family to agree about the responsibilities involved in a delay made unanimous voting at the UN seem more likely.

Justin moved on. "Do you also want to take the risk that an agreement reached now may be broken in a few years' time because one of you has changed their mind? If your answer to that is 'yes' you're more of a gambler than I am." Justin was in fact a born gambler, but had no problem with economy of truth when circumstances required it.

Justin felt it was time to put pressure on his audience. "My own view is you should sell now for the best price possible. I think I can get you full market value now, perhaps more. What do you say to that?"

Henrietta was the first to break the silence. "I think we should keep the set as a whole and sell it. I'd prefer to sell it sooner rather than later — I'm not getting any younger." She paused, before adding "I'd understand if the next generation wants to delay, but I'm interested that you think you can get full market value now, perhaps more."

"I can't agree with you, Henrietta," was the immediate challenge from Natasha. "We should delay a sale. Walter was convinced the set would go up a lot in the next few years." She turned to Anne. "You're the next generation. What do you think? You agree to delay, don't you?"

Anne replied she'd prefer to hear views from everyone before making up her mind, a response guaranteed (or calculated, thought Anthony) to rile her mother.

Caroline knew that, as a recent arrival on the scene, her views would count for little, but she couldn't remain silent. "I'm new to all this and I've decided that whatever I get from the set should go to Graham." This clearly came as a surprise to Graham. He smiled at Caroline as she continued, "But I must say one thing. Do not break up the set. If you do it'll be destruction of the worst kind, a real loss. The art world will never forgive you."

"Thanks for that, Caroline" said Graham, "really appreciated. I agree we should keep the set together, but think we should delay the sale for a few years to get a better price." Graham was looking his brother straight in the eye when saying this. If he was serving his revenge on a dish, it was on one of the coldest dishes imaginable.

Claire rose to the bait and her response was immediate. "I don't agree to a delay and nor does Peter. We've no idea how long to wait before selling. We should sell now. The extra cash will help all of us." Peter nodded in agreement but said nothing. The strain on him was beginning to tell, and he knew his voice would betray that to the family.

Anthony then stepped in. "I want you all to know that I will be giving whatever I receive from the set into the general pot. I can't benefit personally — the rules of my profession prohibit that — and it's right that all of you should take the benefit." Anthony failed to add that, even if he had been able to benefit, he would have declined in view of the tensions in the family. He would have been caught in a crossfire which would make polarisations over Brexit look like a walk in the park. "What I can say is I've talked to Justin about the set and he has an idea about how to secure the very best price now. I urge you to listen to him." With those words he handed back to Justin.

"I suggest you sell the set now," continued Justin "but in a different way from usual. Since first talking to Anthony I've tested the market privately and there are buyers out there prepared to pay a really good price now. The set is recognised by experts as unique and valuable. I have three, possibly four potential buyers lined up and I know they're good for the money. Each of them wants the set. There is competition between them already." Seeing that he had the attention of the room, he moved swiftly on. "So how do you get the best price now? I think it's by holding a private online auction — I can set up a website dedicated to the sale, with the selected potential buyers able to bid online. We'd be able to visit the website, but only as spectators."

"But why should an auction like that be worth it now?"

The interruption came from Graham, and Justin answered him. "It's the kind of auction I'm suggesting which has the best chance of success. I'm suggesting a Dutch Auction". Seeing some puzzled faces, Justin explained what he meant. "That's an auction where the auctioneer sets the initial asking price way above what the market value is likely to be. The asking price is then reduced in stages until someone bids, and it's that first bid that wins the auction. There's obviously a reserve price below which no sale is possible, but the bidders have no idea what the reserve price is."

Justin pressed home his point. "In my experience, for unique items such as your chess set you'll achieve a much better price by this method than by a standard auction, where you start low and bids increase until the highest bidder wins. You have a unique work of art, a true one-off, and the owner of it will feel they are the market leader."

Anthony was impressed by Justin's powers of persuasion, but would the Hecht family agree? He jumped in before anyone could disagree. "I think Justin's suggestion is the best option for all of you. Delay will achieve nothing, apart from provoking disagreement between you about what to do. If Justin's right, you'll have cash, a lot of it, which you wouldn't otherwise have. You have to pay tax on the value of the set now anyway and that will use up all the cash there is in Walter's estate at the moment — you'd be left with a valuable asset but no cash. A sale will produce the extra cash," he paused for effect, "and is the only real option for you."

Anthony had stuck his neck out, but defended his views. The arguments in the room continued and Anthony let them run on, knowing that even the most argumentative soul runs out of steam (and bystanders lose the will to live) when confronted with implacable opposition.

The task for Anthony was to interrupt at just the right moment, at a point somewhere between fatigue and exhaustion for the family members so intent on voicing their views. After a few more minutes he judged the moment to be right and raised his voice for the first time that evening, to plead, "You really must reach a decision or we'll be here all night." He had certainly gained the attention of the room, and he then played his final card. "I suggest you hold the Dutch Auction as Justin suggests and try to sell the whole set now, but have a high reserve price. If that's not reached, you can take the set off the market and sell it in a few years' time. Justin can advise what he thinks the high reserve should be."

A few objections, red herrings, flying insults and false starts later, they had reached agreement. Reluctance and prejudice had given way to practicality (although with more than a hint of avarice). Justin would hold the Dutch Auction online a week from today. Anyone who wanted could come to his office to view it. He would decide on the reserve price the day before the auction.

Once all the family members had departed, Justin and Anthony were left together in the private room. Both felt a sense of relief with a touch of optimism, but tainted by realism.

Leo served them a glass of wine each, which they raised in a toast to Dutch courage.

Chapter Twenty-two
Walter

Today was the day of the auction. Justin had put in a superhuman effort to make it a success, lining up four bidders through their UK agents. Two bidders were from the Far East, one from the USA and one from Europe, but he did not know the identity of the bidders, only that their agents had vouched unreservedly for them and had proved they had sufficient funds to participate. If the auction failed it would not be through a lack of preparation.

The auction would be online. The asking price would appear on screen, starting at £2 million. The first to lodge an electronic bid would win the day and, at that moment, the screen would show that the successful bid had been made. Justin had fixed the reserve price at £950,000, which he felt was high but that was what the family, through the tortuous process a week ago, had wanted.

Anthony and Henrietta joined Justin at his office in the West End a few minutes before midday, the scheduled auction time. All the others had said they would watch online but at home. Apart from reassuring one another how exceptional the chess set was, there was little talk in Justin's room prior to the auction; pre-match nerves of an artistic kind, heightened by years of family tension.

The large screen on the wall formed the dramatic backdrop to the event, coming to life at midday exactly to show a figure — £2 million — and a short statement. "The indicated price will reduce automatically by £50,000 every ten seconds. The first to lodge an electronic bid will be the successful buyer." Each bidder was logged into the auction site, a fact confirmed for all to see onscreen.

'The auction will begin in ten seconds,' announced the message onscreen. And it then began.

'Two million pounds' appeared onscreen, together with a numerical display counting down the seconds. After ten seconds and no bid having been made, '£1,950,000' appeared. And then £1,900,000, then £1,850,000 and so on down to £1,600,000. Justin was wondering whether his advice had been over-optimistic, but it was too late to worry about that now. £1,550,000 came and went, as did £1,500,000. And then it happened — a bid at £1,450,000, confirmed onscreen as being from Bidder 4. The silence in Justin's room was deafening, until broken by a vehement "YES!" from Anthony, echoed by Justin. Henrietta sat in shock, not to say disbelief, at the extraordinary result.

They agreed a celebratory lunch at Messanto was the next priority and Anthony called Leo then and there to book it for later at his usual table.

***

Others had seen the auction in their very different ways.

Natasha had returned to Northern Ireland by the time of the auction. She had seen nothing to keep her in London, the family having proved unwelcoming. She hadn't expected a red carpet, but to have no carpet at all for her had hit home. She was pleased by the auction result — what a fantastic sale price — and looked forward to hearing from Anthony with her share of the sale proceeds, but she felt a sense of emptiness because that was all she had to look forward to as far as the family were concerned.

Claire was ecstatic at the result. She could now afford to deal with more designers and they could build the conservatory on the back of the house at last. In the same way a runaway train flattens all in its path, she left Peter in no doubt about what would happen to the sale proceeds. This left Peter in no doubt that Albert Hall would need to be active in the very near future.

Caroline and Graham had been out together the evening before the auction. Their relationship was accelerating at a speed they barely realised, relaxing in each other's company and devoting time to finding out more about each other. The nightcap in Caroline's flat in Fulham that evening had led naturally to the bedroom, where their mutual passion had culminated in explosions of pleasure for them both. Neither had headed for the office the following morning and, having overslept, they were still at the flat after a leisurely breakfast when the auction began. They watched it, spellbound, on Caroline's laptop. Once the result was known, Graham insisted they should put a large part of the proceeds into a new business they would run together. They could sort out the details later. The new venture was sealed with a kiss. Or two.

Anne was sitting in the Business Class lounge at Heathrow, waiting for her flight home. She had watched the auction on her iPad and was delighted with the result.

Her bid had been successful.

Anne had inherited her father's business drive and acumen. A few years ago she had understood the way the retail market was going, with a growing emphasis on buying online rather than in store. Putting what little money she had where her mouth was, she had formed a company supplying the software and logistics required for goods to be bought online and then delivered to buyers promptly. She had devoted huge amounts of energy and time to growing the business, and the company's success had attracted the attention of a major player (in other words competitor) in the same market, with huge financial backing from the USA. Anne had resisted the first two takeover bids from the competitor, but the third bid, of just under £11 million, had been too good to ignore. She had taken the money a year or so ago and would remain involved with the business for another year as part of the deal.

Her financial worries behind her, she had been free to indulge in a passion of hers, the art market. She was endowing a new art gallery in Northern Ireland and had seen the chess set as an ideal item to launch the gallery's collection. It was a truly exceptional work of art, lost on most members of the Hecht family. She had no problem in providing them with cash — their need was obviously greater than hers — and above all she had preserved the set for posterity.

She wouldn't reveal she had been the purchaser at auction, at least for now; it would serve no useful purpose. Only Justin was aware of her identity, but he was sworn to secrecy on pain of losing future business from her as she sought more items for the gallery. The truth would come out at some time in the future and she would deal with it then.

Walter had played a greater part in her life than she had recognised before: she had inherited his best characteristics without too many of the troublesome ones. She wished she had known him better.

She raised her champagne glass in a silent toast to her father.

Chapter Twenty-three
Helen

Leo had a soft spot for Helen. She was a regular diner, seated that lunchtime at her usual table towards the front of the restaurant. She was the ideal customer, demanding only when necessary, rather than for the sake of it like some others, and appreciative of the good service invariably offered to her. Today she was with her mother, Venetia, at one of their regular lunches. Leo, helped by Julia who also liked Helen and found her delightful to deal with, made sure the attention mother and daughter received was exactly what was needed.

Helen's approach to life seemed to Leo to be matched by her general manner; unassuming, always well-dressed but in an understated way, and preferring whenever possible to avoid confrontation. Despite this, or perhaps because of it, Leo sensed that Helen needed an extra dimension to her life. His brief conversations with her at the restaurant had revealed she worked hard but had little or no social life to speak of; Leo saw this as a senseless waste and resolved to help her.

Helen enjoyed her visits to Messanto, happy to maintain a low profile and not cause problems for anyone. She and Venetia covered a wide range of subjects over their monthly lunches and, as part of this, Helen was able to catch up, in a relaxed way, with the family history. So much had been left unsaid over the years that Helen encouraged Venetia, now approaching her seventies and with a memory not as clear as a few years ago, to talk about the past. Without this and with no one else to fill in the gaps, the history would be lost.

Helen had learned over time, and in more detail over the lunchtime chats, that her mother had been married twice, the first time to a man who had been not only the first to take her to bed, but also unfortunately the first to make her pregnant. At the insistence of her father, who had shotgun at the ready, Venetia had married him and a son, James, had been born a few weeks after the wedding. The marriage had ended in divorce some four years later, and Venetia had remarried almost immediately. Helen had arrived eighteen months later, after a planned pregnancy Helen's mother had assured her.

This sequence of events, designed as it was to keep lawyers and accountants in business, had led to longer-term financial arrangements being set up for the family. Venetia's father, Joseph, a successful businessman in the company he had founded and worked in all his life, had set up a trust with shares in the company and a substantial cash sum, tied up in such a way that no gold-digging man who married his daughter would ever get his hands on any of it. Such was his suspicious mind, it was in fact impossible for any man married to his daughter, whether or not digging for precious metal, to get his hands on one penny of it. The trustees of the trust were Joseph and his solicitor, a man now in his early sixties. They controlled everything and pulled all the purse strings.

The chats with her mother over lunch were always good-natured and it was fascinating for Helen to gain some insight into her family. To achieve success, Joseph had obviously adopted a dictatorial strategy with his staff, derived from the Vlad the Impaler school of consensus: there was no need for him to advertise his business mantra — do as I say or be fired — and he brought the same attitude home with him after work. You ignored his views at your peril. Not helped by being a naturally reserved character, Venetia had been given little say in the way the family lived, let alone about the family's finances. She concentrated on her two children and if there was more than enough to go round, be it cash or food on the table, she was content to look no further.

But for Helen, there was an additional and fundamental element to the lunchtimes with her mother.

Helen needed to understand why she had felt second-best in the family throughout her life. She also needed to see if she could do anything about it. She could not ignore the feeling which had gnawed away at her for years. She would even the score, somehow. It was simply a question of time, but how would she do it?

Venetia, although a caring mother, had no idea that Helen felt that way. If she had suspected it, she would have revealed much less to Helen about the family. Helen was able to ask questions a few at a time over the lunches, without her mother suspecting an underlying theme. There could be no hint of interrogation and Helen's approach was measured with this in mind. Mother and daughter were very similar characters, preferring a quieter approach to their lives.

Venetia's first husband, an attractive but immature man, had melted away into the distance at the first sign of trouble in the marriage. Joseph had made him feel as useful as a teetotaller at a wine tasting and had treated him as cannon fodder, being incapable of giving as good as he got, although any attempt on his part to try anything so rash would have failed utterly. Joseph's technique when confronted with a problem was to use a sledgehammer at least twice the size needed to crack it. No money found its way to him from the family purse and, as an unemployed and (unfortunately for him) unambitious individual, his prospects in the family were dead in the water, although they might not even have floated in the first place. Venetia had known the marriage was a mistake but did not have the will to resist her father. She had felt a sense of relief when her husband had left one night with the Spanish au pair, leaving a note to say he would be in touch again soon about a divorce, probably from Malaga.

Venetia's second husband was a professional musician, whose skills were increasingly recognised in the music world. Although gainfully employed in a London-based orchestra, his pay was meagre by comparison with other professions. Despite this, he had won the family's approval; he was intelligent, talented and had a streak of ambition, but offered no threat to the power base of the family. He could paddle his own musical canoe and was happy to do this. After Helen's arrival, Venetia's married life had settled down.

One point sprang loud and clear from the chats. Venetia had not appreciated that her total exclusion from decisions affecting the family and its finances had been deliberate. Joseph and his solicitor ruled the financial side, and she had been grateful for the family trust they managed. All her and her husband's considerable living expenses had been paid; the children lacked for nothing; there was no shortage of luxury holidays, plus there was a spacious roof over their heads in a fashionable part of London. All this was financed from the trust and Venetia and her husband had no reason to complain. Why would she poke a stick into the wasps' nest, even if sometimes she might have liked to know more.

Venetia would have professed surprise had Helen suggested that James had always come first in the pecking order. Whilst Helen had been to average primary and secondary schools, James had profited from the most exclusive, not to say costly, education that money could buy. His academic performance had left much to be desired, but his transition to a role in the family company had been automatic once it had been agreed he should not trouble any university admission tutors. By contrast, it had always been made clear to Helen that there was no place for her in the man's world of the family business. She should make her own way in life.

James had led a life of superhuman extravagance, all financed from the trust which had also paid for his wedding to Amanda. Their honeymoon had been the stuff of legend. Its length meant it was easier to list the five-star hotels in the Caribbean they had not visited, rather than those they had visited. On their return, they had been presented with the keys to a house in Chelsea, again financed from the trust. One silver spoon in the mouth had been replaced by a full canteen of them.

No such extravagance had been offered to Helen. Her schooling had been adequate, at a boarding school in Sussex which educated girls to be adornments rather than leaders. She had achieved three good A Levels despite the efforts of her teachers, but the family finances apparently did not run to a university place for her. After leaving school she had found herself a job as a trainee accounts clerk, numeracy being her strongest skill.

Helen's first attempt to introduce a boyfriend into the mix had resulted in his being subjected to a course of aversion therapy by the family. A more successful way to strangle a relationship at birth did not exist and Helen was reduced to telling potential suitors that her family lived abroad. She had been given the keys to a flat in Battersea, in marked contrast to James and Amanda's mansion — that estate agents were christening unfashionable Battersea as South Chelsea at the time was no more than cold comfort.

The six-year age gap between her and James meant they had spent little time together when in their teens or early twenties, and they had not made much effort to become closer since then. Their lives were taking completely different directions, and they might as well have occupied different hemispheres for all the contact they had. There was not much Helen could do about it, or wanted to do, at least for the moment. She had found James's wife, Amanda, uncommunicative on the few occasions she had met her, but that could well have been down to James's indifference towards his sister.

Helen had received a small but regular allowance from the trust, but even that had reduced dramatically without warning a few years before. From something James had said, it seemed his extravagant lifestyle had also been curtailed by an unwelcome shortage of cash from the trust, but he was more secure financially having recently become sales director of the family company.

The family's intentional — it was beyond casual — indifference towards her and her prospects in life had rankled, but Helen had been prepared to postpone her reaction to it until such time as she was sure of her ground. 'Don't get mad, get even' was one of the few lessons she had learned from her schooling.

She was now ready.

Her thinking had crystallised when looking through Joseph's papers. Venetia was terrified of figures and, following Joseph's death a couple of years before, had relied on Helen to manage her finances and keep a watchful eye on her investments. Joseph had controlled all the finances in his lifetime, at the same time keeping impeccable records. James was involved in a limited way, making sure Venetia's medical treatments were paid for, but he was not involved to any greater extent — there was a reason he had never been considered for the role of finance director at the company.

Venetia had retained all Joseph's papers despite his death, being reluctant to throw away records which she did not understand and which were so closely associated with him. Venetia had asked Helen to look through the papers — which were voluminous and taking up too much space, many of them pre-dating digital technology and cloud-based storage — to see what might be thrown away and what should be kept. Joseph's immaculate record-keeping had proved a bonus to Helen, from which she now hoped to reap the benefit.

Following today's lunch with her mother, Helen was due to meet the solicitor who had worked so closely with Joseph over the years. She had some questions for him. She wanted answers. She would get them. She had no more than one glass of wine with lunch before setting off for her meeting, having said goodbye to her mother and promising she would be in touch soon.

***

The offices of Townfield & Son, Solicitors, were in a neat square in Knightsbridge. A brochure in their reception area revealed there were two partners in the firm, Gavin Townfield and his son Sebastian, who provided a 'dedicated and efficient service to their clients, at reasonable cost'. Helen looked round in vain for a dish of salt from which to take a pinch, but was interrupted by the receptionist who announced that Gavin would see her now.

Helen had met Gavin only once before, at Joseph's funeral. He was a man in his early sixties, full of self-confidence and whose waistline revealed a carefree attitude towards his diet. He had been indifferent towards her at the funeral, but Helen was determined to get his attention this time. After the customary preliminaries, he began the discussion. "What can I do for you?"

Helen's reply was equally broad. "Can you please tell me something about the family trust my grandfather, Joseph, set up all those years ago?"

Gavin's confident response was to launch into a prepared but bland description of the trust and the way it worked. Joseph and he had looked after it as trustees, paying out money to the various members of the family as the beneficiaries. Accounts were drawn up every year to show what had happened in the period. Helen was aware of this — it was her reading of the accounts amongst Joseph's papers which had prompted her decision to meet Gavin — but to seem unfamiliar with trust accounts served her purpose better.

"So you and Joseph took all the decisions?" asked Helen.

"Not all decisions," he replied. "We used specialist advisers for any stock exchange investments." On being pressed, Gavin revealed that the trust had been set up initially with some shares in the family company, together with cash which had been invested in the stock market. Joseph had always had strong views about how the money should be invested, and the investment advisers had been content to follow his directions so long as they did not depart too much from the model portfolio they would usually put together. When pressed further by her, Gavin admitted he had gone along with it all. He also revealed that he was now the only trustee, following Joseph's death: he alone controlled everything.

Helen detected a note of irritation creeping into Gavin's voice as he was put more firmly on the spot by her probing. Pleased that his self-confidence was ebbing away, she moved to a different tack.

She knew the accounts showed a huge disparity between the amounts paid out for James and the amounts for her. Gavin would know that too and so, to add to his discomfort, she asked, "My brother's a beneficiary of the trust?" Gavin nodded in agreement. "Can you tell me how you reached decisions to pay money out to either of us?"

"I was guided by Joseph," was Gavin's guarded reply. "He was in much closer contact with the family than me and so it seemed sensible to rely on him."

Gavin's comments had the ring of truth. It had been difficult to contradict Joseph, a man of strong views whose sole concession to equality had been to seek, offend and destroy as many women as men on his path to success. He had not believed in equality of opportunity or, it must be said, equality of anything, for females. Gavin's increasing discomfort at her approach showed he recognised the disparity between her and her brother's treatment.

Her confidence growing, she decided to move on.

"I was paid an allowance from the trust, as I believe was my brother, but that's all but dried up now. What caused that?"

"Some investments were more successful than others," came the defensive reply. "The trust was advised to buy shares in dot.com companies, but nearly all that money was lost when the boom went bust. We held shares in banks, some of which also went bust in 2008 and haven't really recovered since. The family company wasn't doing as well as expected, mainly because of the Brexit uncertainty. There was much less available for the beneficiaries."

Helen knew this sorry tale was partly true, but also knew Gavin was holding back the full story. She had accepted long ago that investments could go down as well as plummet in value, but it was time to dig deeper.

"The accounts show a number of loans being made. More than half a million pounds in all. Who received them?"

"They were loans for investment by specialists — that's how they're described in the accounts — but they mostly proved unsuccessful." Gavin's hesitation in replying gave way to shock as Helen put her next question to him.

"But weren't you one of the specialists who received the loans?"

Gavin knew at that moment that Helen had information far beyond the anodyne statements in the accounts. He was struggling, unable to marshal his defences as he could only guess at the extent of her knowledge.

His reluctance to reply was seized on by Helen. "Well, weren't you? What happened to the money?"

Gavin's silence spoke volumes, his face ashen. Helen pressed home her advantage. "Let me put you out of your misery. I know from reading Joseph's papers that he wanted to give you something extra, to recognise your hard work over the years. You'd helped him to build up the company and reinforced his success in a major way." Gavin sat motionless as Helen twisted the knife a little more. "He couldn't reward you through the company — the auditors and finance people would have spotted it straight away — and so he used the trust. The loans, at first sight for investment, were no such thing, that's what it looks like from the personal papers of his I've read."

Helen paused to draw breath. Her patience in waiting until she had the ammunition she needed was paying off. She decided to push the knife home.

"I have a real problem with what you've done, Gavin. You did everything Joseph told you to do. You favoured my brother without a second thought. You let Joseph choose investments, most of which went pear-shaped. You took the loans and used them for your own purposes. I've lost out at every turn, all thanks to your supine attitude to Joseph." Helen was surprised at her own fluency but carried on. "You also ignored my mother, never consulting her. How on earth could you decide to pay out anything to me or my mother without the basic courtesy of consulting either of us?"

Gavin was exercising his right to remain silent.

"I'm not sure what to do about it. Does your son know how you conduct your business? He's a partner, after all. I'm not sure whether to sue you," Helen was almost finished, "but I *am* sure the Law Society would take a dim view of what you've done, particularly with the loans."

Helen paused for effect, before adding, "Unless of course they *are* loans and you repay them, with interest." Gavin's continuing silence was more deafening than golden.

She stood up to end the discussion, saying, "You have a week to repay the loans, with interest. If you don't pay, I'll report you to the appropriate authorities." She wanted to add she'd like to report him to some inappropriate authorities as well if she could find them but, to Helen's mind, this particular lily was to be nurtured rather than gilded.

"You must also resign as a trustee," was her parting shot as she left the meeting room.

Her mood was upbeat as she left Townfield & Son's offices. This was only the beginning of events which would play out over the next few days, but the meeting had gone as well as she could have hoped.

* * *

It was a week later. Helen was in Messanto, sitting at her usual table. Her guest for lunch had yet to arrive, but for now she was more interested in her laptop — she looked at the screen every few minutes. Would the money arrive?

Leo was attentive, bringing her olives and mineral water to help calm her nerves. He knew something was afoot, but not what it was, only that it was clearly all-consuming for Helen who was usually calm itself. He guessed that strong drink would be needed at some stage over lunch, either to celebrate success or to drown sorrows. He kept a watchful eye on her.

Helen had not been idle in the week since meeting Gavin Townfield. She had taken legal advice from Anthony a few weeks ago, at Leo's recommendation. She had spoken to him again in the last week to make sure what she wanted was possible. She had also spoken to Gavin twice since their meeting, once to tell him what she required him to do, a second time to check he was doing it.

A basic search at the Land Registry had revealed that Gavin owned a freehold house near his office in Knightsbridge, completely free of mortgage. Helen instructed him that, if he didn't have enough cash he should mortgage the house immediately, so that he could pay £600,000 into the trust's account at Townfield & Son. That would repay the loans, with interest. The same sum should then be transferred to her, as a beneficiary of the trust. It was her bank account she was checking every few minutes. Today was the day Gavin had told her he would make the transfer.

She wanted the money to arrive before lunch. Her guest was new to her life. Taking a new-found courage in both hands, she had followed a suggestion from Leo and had met Manmar Consultants for a chat. She had been electrified to meet her former sister-in-law, Amanda, by then divorced from Helen's brother, James, as part of Manmar but they had immediately found a rapport that would have been impossible before the divorce. Amanda understood Helen and what she wanted without the need to ask too many questions.

The result had been an introduction by Manmar to a charming man, much the same age as her and with whom Helen had so far shared a brunch, a visit to the theatre, lunch in a country pub and then, most recently, an evening meal at Messanto. The chemistry between them was there, but this was early days in a relationship they both hoped would develop, with no need to break any sprint records to get there. Today's lunch was another step along the way.

Helen checked the screen again: it was the very moment the money arrived in her account. The look on her face, an ecstatic mixture of triumph and relief, was obvious and she called Leo over to the table. "A glass of that fantastic Italian sparkling wine, what is it again?"

"The Franciacorta?" offered Leo.

"Yes, that's it. A glass for me now thanks, and one for my guest the moment he arrives."

"Of course," replied Leo, as he turned towards the bar to fill the order. "I'll show Mr Townfield to the table as soon as he arrives."

Chapter Twenty-four
Gavin and Sebastian

It is a truth universally acknowledged
that a young lawyer in possession of a good
fortune
must be in want of a life

This misquotation from Jane Austen had played an important part in Sebastian Townfield's life. Printed and framed, it sat on his office desk as a constant reminder of what might have been. Rather than an opening line, it had been the final gift from his fiancée for whom the extraordinary amount of time Sebastian spent at work, and the stress of it, had been one of several steps too far. "Our relationship is going nowhere. In fact it's non-existent," had been her biting assessment as she handed him the engagement ring with one hand — "You can have that back for a start," — and the framed misquotation, with M*ore Prejudice than Pride* according to her, with the other. "I refuse to marry an office and that father of yours is impossible. I'm exhausted and so is my patience. I'm leaving you." With those words she had fled Sebastian's life, leaving him with some home truths to go with the shattered dreams.

Sebastian was determined not to make the same mistakes again, but that was easier said than done. His father, Gavin, had perfected a shy tenacity — his instinctive shyness was mistaken by some as indifference — combined with an addiction to the practice of the law which was given to very few. Near-perfection unfortunately reared its head for Gavin as well: his legal analysis was excellent, but his outward appearance of confidence was all too fragile, readily punctured by a persistent opponent. This had resulted in him starting his own solicitors' practice with one major client, Joseph, together with the family company which he had formed.

Joseph's powers of persuasion, founded as they were on intransigence, would make even the toughest negotiator admit defeat, and Gavin was the perfect advisor for Joseph — a first-rate lawyer, but one whose skills could be moulded to achieve the result desired by Joseph.

After obtaining a good degree from Durham University, Sebastian had trained with a medium-sized law firm in Holborn and had passed the exams to enable him to practice. He had then encountered an obstacle which had proved impossible to overcome. No firm of lawyers was prepared to consider him as a serious prospect because his father was a well-known lawyer keeping a seat warm for his son.

Nothing Sebastian said had persuaded the firms that he despised nepotism or that he suspected the best

146

recipe for failure was to work for a parent. As a result, he had taken up the only route open to him, to join his father, but he had made it a condition that the two of them should operate in different areas of law. That was how Sebastian aimed to preserve an otherwise good relationship with his father.

The two of them had worked hard to succeed, but Gavin's addiction to long working hours had proved catching. Sebastian soon found himself working twelve hours a day, sometimes more. Earlier in his working life he had found time to meet, go out with and then propose to the girl of his dreams. She had accepted, but it had come as a surprise to him when she had left him a few months later, handing him the framed misquotation. The symptoms of a collapsing relationship had escaped Sebastian entirely, leaving her with a bewildered feeling of isolation.

As time went on, Sebastian spent more time in the office than out of it. His free time involved her, but not frequently enough for someone who wanted to build a life with her partner. There was always something more important for him to do, although his reluctance to be involved in the planning for their wedding day was entirely understandable, given that his future mother-in-law's conversation was based on not hearing him at the first time of asking. His fiancée's complaints to father and son had fallen on completely deaf ears. She complained to Sebastian that he should forget what he had obviously learned at the Henry VIII School of

Marriage Guidance. In her final argument with Gavin she had used words which were more forceful than picturesque, complaining amongst other things that Sebastian's conception must have been immaculate, if not a miracle, given the amount of time Gavin spent in the office.

His fiancée's departure had, ironically, left Sebastian more time to devote to work. It was challenging work, which he enjoyed, and the clients, mainly Joseph and his company, were delighted with the service offered by Townfield & Son, as the firm had been named once Sebastian had become a partner in the business. Father and son worked well together and had a strong relationship, Gavin working on the corporate side, Sebastian on the contractual and employment side.

They had also found common ground away from the law.

The two of them shared one passion in particular, a love of Italian food and wine. When time allowed, usually well into the evening, they would meet at Messanto at their usual table to sample the delights on offer. Gavin headed straight for the cured meats — beef carpaccio or Parma ham. Whilst Sebastian enjoyed venison ravioli — a speciality of the house — or a Caprese salad, a mouth-watering combination of mozzarella cheese, tomatoes and basil. The white wines from the north-east of Italy, the Alto Adige in particular, were outstanding and were the perfect accompaniment for seafood dishes such as spaghetti vongole or steamed sea bass, whilst the reds from Piedmont, a Barbera perhaps, were a typical recommendation from the sommelier to accompany a main course of rack of lamb, or a pasta dish such as pappardelle with a duck ragout. Messanto chose its wines carefully, and the sommelier was only too happy to serve any diner who so clearly knew their glass from their elbow.

It was over evening meals at Messanto that Sebastian had got to know his father best, but it had been over the last couple of years, since Joseph's death, that Sebastian had truly recognised not only his father's strengths but also, inevitably, his weaknesses.

Joseph had been an all-pervasive client, using Gavin's strengths as a lawyer but preying on his weakness as someone who extended the boundaries of indecision — Gavin couldn't make up his mind whether he was indecisive. Gavin was able to see both sides of an argument, frequently being in two minds (both of them, it must be said, usually right) about the solution.

Sebastian recognised the need to support his father and even, as his experience grew, to point him in the right direction. Sebastian had a toughness of mind which his father lacked. Gavin's experience complemented Sebastian's inexperience. The combination of the two of them was stronger than the constituent parts individually.

Decisions came most easily to Gavin as he relaxed at his usual table at Messanto. He had no problem deciding what to eat or drink, nor in confiding in

Sebastian about the demands of being a lawyer. Gavin had lost his wife, Sebastian's mother, to breast cancer ten years before and had managed his grief by devoting more and more time to the business. It had also opened the door to a much closer relationship with his only child, Sebastian, an opportunity father and son had seized as a result of their mutual loss. He had hinted to Sebastian in the past about how difficult Joseph had been, but had stopped short of the full story — until only a few days ago. The two of them had met at Messanto for an evening meal on the day Gavin had met Helen. Gavin's choice of wine to go with the main course, an outstanding Nebbiolo from Piedmont which he chose only rarely, had forewarned Sebastian that something unusual was afoot.

It was in the conversation at the table that evening that Sebastian had first heard of the loans made by the trust to Gavin. As the story unfolded, it became clear to Sebastian that his father, who had stressed to his son countless times that professional honesty was everything, had been steamrollered into accepting something that ran contrary to his every instinct. Joseph's insistence on paying over the money had been irresistible, and Gavin's protestations had been ignored. The extra payments had been mentioned in the past, but Gavin had always described them to Sebastian as being part of the trust. True to form, Gavin had been undecided what to do with the money and had taken not one penny of it for himself.

Gavin's report on his meeting with Helen earlier that day, uncomfortable as the meeting had been for him but sparing no detail, enabled the two of them to work out their options. They talked at length, into a second bottle of the Nebbiolo, and agreed on what should be done. The money should be paid within the week stipulated by her. Sebastian was to talk it all through with Helen when he next met her. She had told him of her intended chat with his father, but had avoided any details. He now knew why. He already had a lunch date fixed with her, at Messanto for a week's time. He would meet her as planned, although he was troubled by conflicting emotions, a close relationship with his father as against his developing relationship with Helen. He knew that he alone was able to resolve the conflict, but he also knew he only had a week to work out how.

Leo had watched father and son over time, recognising the danger signs in Sebastian's life. Once again, minimal social life and an ever-increasing workload. At Leo's suggestion, Sebastian had made time to meet Manmar one evening at Messanto. Helen had then appeared on Sebastian's horizon, a result that had brought a smile to Leo's lips.

Chapter Twenty-five
Helen

And so it was that Sebastian joined Helen at Messanto exactly a week later. Her most welcoming smile greeted him, as did a glass of Franciacorta as he sat down. They raised their glasses in a toast to each other, and the warmth so obviously radiating from her would, he realised, melt his defences in no time. He also knew that to feign ignorance about the reason for her celebration would wreck the occasion. He decided to come straight to the point.

"I know why we're celebrating, and that's great. I've had long chats with my father in the last week." Her smile slipped a little at this, but she didn't interrupt. "I know what happened at your meeting with him, and I also know the money should have arrived in your account by now." She nodded as he pressed on, "I want you to understand what happened in the past, and what we're going to do about it. Let's choose some food and we can talk some more."

Once Leo had taken their order for both food and wine, Sebastian was able to continue, "My father and Joseph worked well together and the family company thrived as a result. Joseph was overbearing, one of his least endearing characteristics, but it led to business success. He wanted my father to share in the success financially and wouldn't take no for an answer when my father refused the offers of what were really bonuses. He paid the money over to my father anyway."

He could see that he still had Helen's attention. He took a sip from his glass and pressed on. "That left my father with a dilemma. He didn't want the money, but there was no point in returning it because Joseph had threatened to fire my father as the company's lawyer if that happened."

"But that's ridiculous," Helen retorted. "He should have returned the money — so what if he lost the company as a client?"

"Like it or not, and my father didn't like it, the firm would have folded. Without Joseph's company as a client there weren't enough other clients to pay the bills."

Helen and Sebastian looked at each other across the table, each unwilling to push the other much further, but Sebastian was in too deep to give up. He pressed on, "My father knew that Joseph's insistence on funding your brother's lifestyle was unfair to you, but again couldn't risk losing the company as a client. He just hoped something would turn up, so that he could balance the books between you later." Aware he was laying bare his father's weaker side, Sebastian moved swiftly on. "My father didn't touch the money, except to invest it. 'Out of sight, out of mind' was his approach;

he put it in something that would look after itself, producing no income and providing no tax headaches. He could invest it and then forget about it. He invested the money in gold and it's sat there ever since."

Helen immediately thought it was unwise to invest in such a risky commodity, but said nothing. She drank from her glass, hoping Sebastian wasn't digging himself into a deeper hole. She knew he was honest. The question was whether his father was too. As if reading her mind, Sebastian carried on, "You may not like the thought of gold as an investment, but it's turned out to be a fantastic success — it's doubled in value since my father first invested in it about five years ago. He thinks of it as part of the trust, and always has done. He also thinks you should take it all now, not just the £600,000 he's paid to you. It's part of bringing you up to the same level of benefit as your brother."

Sebastian sat back, having said enough for the moment. He had more to say, but he was conscious of how alluring Helen looked and he found it more and more difficult to concentrate on the story he was telling.

Helen remained silent, lost in thought. Although intrigued by what Sebastian was saying, she was conscious of how attractive he looked and she found it more and more difficult to concentrate on his story.

They both turned their attention to the food which, as luck would have it, Leo had just brought to the table. Townfield & Son's troubles were shelved for a while, and the two of them ate in silence whilst they collected their thoughts, but their pulse rates didn't slow down at all. Their lunchtime choice of mixed grilled fish to share was ideal, enabling them to smile — was it a bit nervously? — at each other. Sebastian's revelations had, unexpectedly, broken down a barrier between them that neither of them had realised existed until it was no longer there. The hidden shackles had been removed.

It was Helen who took the bull by the horns, casting her usual caution aside. She welcomed his interest in her — the signs were obvious — and she realised her feelings for him went way beyond lunchtime chats. She knew that to let the opportunity pass would be frustrating, in every sense of the word. Consigning subtlety to the dustbin, she heard herself say, "We've talked enough about the trust for now, but would you like to see the flat which the trust bought me? We could go for a walk in Battersea Park which is nearby and then have a coffee in the flat.".

Sebastian accepted the invitation with what he hoped wasn't too much alacrity, but he found it difficult to hide his enthusiasm. They exchanged smiles as their eyes met, and neither looked away. Leo felt like an intruder as he brought the bill. He left it on the side rather than ruin the moment for them.

They left the restaurant arm-in-arm, finding a cab easily to take them over Chelsea Bridge towards Helen's flat, which was on the top floor of a block overlooking Battersea Park. As the cab pulled up the heavens opened, drenching them both as they raced for the entrance door to the building. They laughed at the thought of going for a walk, agreeing they would have coffee in the flat first and wait for the weather to clear.

Helen opened the door to the flat, saying, "Give me your coat and I'll hang it up to dry," as he followed her in. He walked around the flat, its main attraction being a great view over the park. He also admired the comfortable furniture and general warm ambience. After a while he realised Helen was taking her time hanging up the wet coats. Right on cue, he heard her voice behind him. "How do you like your coffee?" He turned round and their eyes locked. She was wearing a coffee-coloured robe guaranteed to make him forget about coffee. He felt a surge of desire at the sight of her, even more so as the robe opened easily to his touch. He kissed her, gently at first but more passionately as she responded with an eagerness she had long forgotten. She led him to her bedroom and it was only a matter of moments before they were both naked on the bed. Their desire took over and his probing embrace, tender but insistent at the same time, quickly saw their bodies rising and falling in unison. His tenderness gave way to urgency, but with perfect timing as they accelerated and reached the heights together. They shared the most intimate of smiles, their sexual release complete as they dozed in each other's arms.

It was a couple of hours later that Helen awoke. She found herself alone in the bed, but she could hear Sebastian's voice from the living room where it sounded like he was on his mobile. Her desires had been rekindled that afternoon in a way she had not thought possible. She lay back in the sheets and smiled to herself as she recalled their lovemaking. She also thought of her reputation as someone who was more timid than daring: she enjoyed her new-found confidence in being desired, and desiring in return. From now on she would ignore toys when playing — she would find the nearest matchbox.

Sebastian's call seemed to be taking for ever. She put on her silk dressing-gown and found him sitting on the sofa, wearing only his boxer shorts. He was concentrating intensely on the call which was with someone called Anthony. Her attempts to catch his attention failed, so she loosened the dressing-gown a little… and then a little more. His eyes widened. He wrapped up the call a little too quickly. "Thanks, Anthony. I'll be in touch to confirm the arrangements."

As she approached him she could see he had risen, manfully, to the occasion. He tried to speak. "You'll need your laptop, I've got something to tell y…" but she cut him short, whispering in his ear, "I've found my laptop, I think," as she sat astride him, easing herself down. She kissed him, her eyes smiling all the while. They luxuriated in their desires, her movements growing in intensity. His eyes were lost to the moment, his cries of pleasure were echoed by her as she drove them to a climax which consumed them both, utterly.

Neither had the energy, physical or emotional, to do more than collapse in a contented sprawl on the sofa. Whatever Sebastian had tried to tell her could wait, the longer the better from her point of view.

She realised she had met extreme sexual desire — was it lust? — for the first time in her life.

Better late than never, she thought.

And never better.

***

The following morning found Sebastian on his way to see Anthony. There was legal business to be discussed. He would meet Anthony alone first, with Helen due to join them later. As he walked towards Anthony's office in the morning sunshine, he recalled the events of the previous day. He had fallen for Helen, hook, line and sinker all firmly in place. Nothing in their time together before yesterday had even hinted at her inner feelings. She had awoken latent desire in him, although he wondered idly if, at the current phenomenal rate, he would be more likely to end up in A and E than anywhere else. A problem to be welcomed he decided, as he waited to see Anthony.

His conversation with Anthony went as they had hoped, and Helen then joined them as planned. Anthony welcomed them both and then moved on quickly to the main business. He directed his remarks at Helen to begin with, "I've had a good discussion with Sebastian and — you may not know this — with his father as well. The upshot is that Townfield & Son will become part of my firm once the admin details have been sorted out. Their business will become part of our business and we agree that gives us huge opportunities to grow in the legal market." Anticipating her question, he added, "You'll want to know how that affects you. My firm will take over the trust as a client but, more important, Gavin will retire as a trustee and will be replaced by me and another partner from my firm." He understood the quizzical look on her face as he continued, "We need to draw a line under the past for the trust. The main purpose of today is to talk that through and decide where we go from here."

"So what does that mean exactly?" queried Helen. "The trust has been dead to me for quite a while, but it's going to revive, is it? How will that work? I've been ignored for years, but I'm now centre stage?" There was a distinct edge to her voice as she posed her questions, all delivered with a steely glare.

Before Anthony could answer, the bitterness in Helen's voice surfaced. "Thanks to Joseph and the trust, yes, I've had a roof over my head for which I'm grateful, but I've had little or no money to live on. I've had a series of jobs, above all trying to make ends meet whilst my brother swans around as sales director of the company, with mixed results I might add. I earn my own living. History has taught me to ignore anyone who tells me my troubles are over."

Anthony had expected some complaints from Helen, but her depth of feeling took him by surprise. He kept going, trying hard to sound sympathetic rather than patronising. "I'm sorry, but I can't undo what's been done in the past. What's done is done. My role is to help you in the future and the first step is to provide you with some financial support. That will also mean you and your brother benefit equally over time."

Helen's reaction was blunt. "As far as I'm concerned, that means giving my brother nothing more from the trust, ever. What's in the trust anyway?"

"There's a little cash, there are the shares in the private company and, there's the gold," replied Anthony. "The company is sound, not overborrowed. It will recover as the business climate improves, but that's some way down the line. The ideal solution would be for the company to be taken over at some stage, but not yet."

She found Anthony's view reassuring, but decided not to tell him, at least for now. He had no way of knowing that Helen's knowledge of accounting, together with the picture revealed by Joseph's private papers, had led her to the same conclusion. She had used the few pennies she had received from the trust wisely, living within her modest means and qualifying as a chartered accountant specialising in forensic analysis — shorthand for spotting fraud. She had lived too near the breadline for comfort, although she had been grateful for the Battersea flat; without it she would have found it impossible to qualify as a professional.

Softening her approach and moving the subject on, she asked "And what's going to happen to the gold?"

"The idea is to sell it, which we'll be doing as soon as we can. Once we've received the proceeds, there'll be quite a sum left over, even after paying expenses and some tax which is due."

"And what will you do with the proceeds then?"

"We'll pay them over to you" said Anthony, adding "and they should amount to something like half-a-million pounds."

It took all her composure not to smile at this. Anthony had played his hand well, but now was not the moment for her to look too pleased. She had no idea that gold had increased in value so much over time, checking the price of gold had never featured on her to-do list. For the first time in her life she was solvent, comfortably, with more than a little to spare. She knew that her brother had spent every single penny of his money from the trust. He was employed by the family company, but his financial horizons were limited. She wished him no harm but knew he would come to regret a lifestyle based on finding new ways to burn through cash at Formula 1 speed. The money from the trust had arrived too early in his life.

She would now be able to pursue one avenue which had not been open to her before.

She had always felt uncomfortable at being dependent on a trust fund. She had never expected too much from it, always promising herself she would put something back if the unexpected happened and she came into money. Well, she thought, the unexpected has come about. She found it ironic that the failure of the trust to provide much more than a roof over her head had forced her to take care of herself but that, now she had a professional career, she had less need for the trust money promised to her. She would give help to others when they needed it most. She would devote a large chunk of the money to charitable projects helping young people up the educational ladder, so that they stood a better chance of a better life.

Combining all this with her burgeoning relationship with Sebastian, was life finally coming together for her? A new start?

Better late than never, she thought.

And never better.

Chapter Twenty-six
Leo

It had been Leo's idea to hold a celebration dinner to mark the tenth anniversary of Messanto opening its doors. He'd run the idea past Julia, who was an enthusiastic supporter, and past several of his regular diners, all of whom had said they would book their usual table for the occasion. He'd also run it past the staff at the restaurant, almost all of whom shared his enthusiasm. The only negative view had come from an experienced waiter who acted as unofficial spokesman for the staff.

"The strain of an evening like that just isn't worth it. Why should we flog ourselves to death producing forty meals simultaneously for that ungrateful crowd?" he complained.

"I think that's unfair," countered Leo. "Yes it'll be hard work, but we can make sure the staff are appreciated if that's what you'd like."

"What do you mean by that?"

"I've had an idea"

"And..."

"We could agree a special rate for the staff working that evening."

"How special?"

"Let's talk about it."

And so the deal had been done, freeing Leo to think about planning the evening. For this he relied on Julia whose choices for celebrations were invariably spot-on. He had interviewed her for a job at Messanto dealing with suppliers on a daily basis, to make sure there was enough food and wine of the right quality available, in the right quantities and at the right time: the restaurant equivalent of a circus juggler. This had been two years ago, but Leo remembered it like it was yesterday. There was an aura to her and her natural confidence had struck him immediately, reinforced by her obvious ability to multi-task; but it was her smile which had knocked him sideways. It had taken his breath away. It had also taken all his strength not to offer her the job before the interview had finished.

Leo's love life up to that moment could best be described by saying Cupid had passed him by — whether because of an empty quiver or blunt arrows, he had no idea — but his interview with Julia had changed all that in an instant. She had accepted his offer of the job; she had followed this a few days later by accepting his invitation to dinner one evening.

Julia's memory of the interview was more blurred. She had liked Leo at first sight and was, she admitted, impressed by his approach at the interview, asking the right questions in the right way. She had also been impressed by the way he looked. She had tried (part of her hoped it was without success) to hide how attracted she was to him. She thought later that, without realising it at the time, she had been interviewed for something more than a job in a restaurant.

Her love life up to then had been erratic at best, veering from the unsuitable to the disappointing and back again. Leo's innate charm had won her heart in no time and she was excited to be with him, sharing a social as well as a business life.

That they were meant for each other was obvious to everyone, except the two of them. They thought it sensible to keep contact in the restaurant down to a minimum because of their working relationship, but even the most short-sighted observers could see through the ruse.

They were constantly in one another's company, but it was a while before Leo realised they should move in together, to share his flat in Pimlico.

"I've had an idea," he said. "Let's live together in my flat. It's ridiculous to have two homes. We spend so much time together."

Although she knew the answer she was going to give, she tested him. "What do you mean, move in together? You must be mad. We see enough of each other as it is and I don't want to be accused of cradle-snatching."

The non-sequitur was typical of Julia, but he played the game. "Come on, I'm only two years younger than you."

That's what you think thought Julia, but to herself as she kept up the struggle. "You do nothing but think about the restaurant and the customers. There's no room left for me in your life, or in what you call a brain."

"It's my heart that counts," was his reply.

"Okay," she said, feigning reluctance. "Let's give it a try, but I'm telling you I'm impossible to live with and have habits that will irritate the hell out of you."

"I'll take the risk if you will" he replied.

"And I have expensive tastes."

They had moved in together a week later.

***

The guests were arriving for the celebration dinner. Julia's organisational skills had proved faultless once again. All the guests had made their food choices online a week ago so that time was not lost during the evening itself. Leo and the sommelier had chosen the wines to be offered with the meal, a four-course extravaganza. Pre-dinner drinks were being served in the private room with a selection of bite-sized canapes.

All of this enabled the guests to mingle before the main event began. Leo and Julia, working as a team, moved around the room making everyone feel welcome, exchanging greetings with the guests and pausing here and there to fill a glass.

Leo took a moment to look around the room. It was a good turnout of regulars and he had been able to give all of them their usual table for the evening. He had realised very early in the ten years that most people liked a kind of consistency when they visited Messanto, they felt appreciated from the word go when shown to their usual table.

Leo truly underestimated the role he played in the lives of others. He concentrated on making sure the food, wine and service were excellent, always. He played down the importance of helping others in their lives beyond Messanto. To him, that was less relevant. It was not in his nature to seek approval or praise for what he did to help his regulars; it would have come as news to him that his combination of priorities had played a major part in making the restaurant a success.

Two scenes were to play out that evening, one attributable to Leo's skills, the other despite them.

A few days ago he had spoken to Alison and Douglas of Branscombe Bank, who were still regulars.

"How's it all going?" he had asked them. "Not an easy time for you."

"No" agreed Douglas immediately. "Oliver dropped us right in it, from a great height. The bank was all over the papers when he was arrested. That died down, but his trial is in a couple of weeks and the whole saga will hit the fan again."

"We're talking about what we should do when it does," added Alison. "Our reputation is at stake and mud can stick."

"I think he's going to plead guilty to fraud," said Douglas, "which means he'll end up with a prison sentence, maybe suspended, plus a major fine."

"At least some good will come of it," smiled Alison. "He'll be disqualified from business for years to come and he'll head off to Cyprus forever. But that won't help the bank much."

"I've had an idea," said Leo thoughtfully. "There's a regular here, his name's Peter Hecht. He works in the PR business and this kind of problem is right up his street. He's coming to the tenth anniversary dinner next week and so are you. Why don't you speak to him? I'm sure he can find time to help you."

And so it was that Douglas, Alison and Peter found themselves in a quiet corner of the private room before the dinner began. They recognised each other, having been nodding acquaintances across a crowded restaurant in the past.

Peter began the main discussion once Leo had filled their glasses. "I've been thinking about what you told me over the 'phone last week and I've got some general ideas about what you should do. The most important thing is to get your story out there first, that's top priority and I can help you with that."

Douglas and Alison nodded in agreement and so he went on, "The next thing is to rebrand the bank. The name Branscombe is tarnished and no amount of polishing will remove the stain." He might have said his current slogan for Branscombe Bank was 'Dung can be Useful' but decided to save that for another occasion.

"This is urgent. How soon can you help us?" asked Douglas, adding, "It might help if you spent a couple of days at the bank next week, so we have a few days before the trial begins."

"I can certainly move my diary around to do that," said Peter.

Leo had once again found a way to introduce the solution to the problem.

***

Leo surveyed the room as the first course was served. To judge by the increasing hubbub of conversation, the evening was a success. All the diners had complimented him on the idea of an anniversary dinner and were entering into the spirit of celebration.

He saw John and Cathy Prowse, celebrating with the buyers of their mews house who were due to move in next week. He would see less of the Prowse family once they had moved to the Sussex coast, but their buyers were enthusiastic consumers of Italian food and wine. He had already earmarked which table would become their usual table.

Sebastian Townfield was transfixed by whatever Helen was saying to him. Leo walked past their table, certain in the knowledge they wouldn't notice him even if he banged a drum. They had eyes only for each other,

169

but in a way that made some of the older guests smile as they recalled a past which they thought they had forgotten.

Mark and Amanda looked on with some satisfaction. They had after all introduced Helen to Sebastian as one of the first clients of Manmar Associates. They spoke to Leo as he walked by, not least to thank him for the part he had played in expanding Manmar's business.

Graham Hecht and Caroline, more clients of Manmar, had booked their usual table for the dinner. Their eyes were locked onto each other, but they at least acknowledged Leo as he moved past them, having refilled their glasses on the way.

Anthony had taken his usual table with two of his partners at the firm, Elizabeth and Clive, plus Gavin Townfield who had just merged his business with theirs. They were discussing the strength of teamwork as against individualism; they agreed that a blend of the two was ideal but almost impossible to achieve for lawyers, whose training lacked even a basic course on 'Modesty for Beginners'. Experience had taught Anthony that his work, in all its guises, required him to transform chalk and cheese into an attractive combination.

Peter Hecht was at his usual table with his wife, Claire, and his mother, Henrietta. All three were beginning to enjoy the evening more than they had expected, although they agreed you could rely on Leo and Julia to set up a good evening. Conversation was never difficult once Claire had warmed up; this usually took no more than a glass or two of wine, and so it was proving that evening as Leo made sure her glass stayed at just the right level to encourage conversation.

Owen Lately had declined the invitation for the evening, both for himself and his wife, Miranda, complaining in his telephone call to Leo that the menu did nothing to help the world. The food on offer was beyond the pale, according to his credo. *His loss*, thought Miranda as she called Leo to set up her next Committee Meeting. *Our gain*, thought Leo when he realised Owen would not be bringing his unique brand of social BO to the party.

Everyone present that evening shared one view. That Leo and Julia worked brilliantly together as a team and that the success of the restaurant, and managing the dinner was just one example, was down to their efforts. The chef and staff were excellent, but it took skill to coordinate the personalities and build the business into the triumph that Messanto had become.

The final course had just been cleared away and so Leo was able to join Julia, the two of them standing towards the back of the restaurant. They were taking a breather before offering coffee, plus something stronger, to the guests. Judging by the amount of food and wine consumed, the evening was a resounding success. Leo and Julia smiled at each other as they stood silently, side by side, sharing in the success of the evening.

They were taken by surprise when Anthony stood up, called for silence by tapping his wine glass and began to speak.

"Don't worry, ladies and gentlemen," he began with a smile on his face "I won't be making a long speech, but you all know why I'm making it." He turned towards Leo and Julia, directing his next remarks at them. "You are the only people who don't know why I'm standing here. You may not realise it, but everyone at this fantastic dinner tonight appreciates the hard work the two of you put in to make Messanto a success. You are helped by an equally fantastic staff, but without your direction I'm not sure the results would be as spectacular."

Murmurs of approval ran round the room as Anthony continued. "We all, every one of us here tonight, wanted to show our appreciation in some way. We thought long and hard about what to do and came up with this." With these words he held up an envelope. "This is a voucher for a holiday for the two of you. Every guest here tonight has contributed towards it and the whole idea is that you should find time for a great holiday away from us all. The voucher means you can choose the holiday — sunshine, winter sports, water sports, safari — whatever you want."

"We want you to enjoy yourselves. Forget about us and have a once-in-a-lifetime break".

Leo and Julia looked at Anthony.

Then at everyone in the room.

Then at each other as they said in perfect unison, "I think we'll make it our honeymoon."